Publisher's Note

After successfully publishing youth-oriented books and getting commendable appreciation from students, teachers and parents alike, V&S Publishers is venturing into the arena of student and job-oriented books with a series of computer books on various important subjects for readers of all ages. Written and presented in lucid language and simple terms, without any computer jargon, these books are an easy-to-follow manual for readers. For the convenience of readers the information is set out in an easy to understand, step-by-step format, with clear illustrations and detailed explanations to accompany each action.

Today we live in a world of computers. The present scenario is that computers are used in every field be it education, business, trade and commerce, home and hobby, or even our ordinary day-to-day life. The importance of computers is an undeniable fact in today's world. In fact, we can't think of a world without computers.

Realising this indisputable fact, we are coming up with the series of **"Comprehensive Computer Learning (CCL)"** books. The series currently includes –

1. Comprehensive Computer Learning (CCL)
2. Comprehensive Computer Learning – A Youngsters' Guide
3. Comprehensive Computer Learning – Microsoft Office 2010
4. Comprehensive Computer Learning – Desktop Publishing (DTP)
5. Comprehensive Computer Learning – Adobe Photoshop
6. Comprehensive Computer Learning – Microsoft Excel 2010
7. Comprehensive Computer Learning – Word 2010
8. Comprehensive Computer Learning – PowerPoint 2010
9. Comprehensive Computer Learning – Publisher, Access & Outlook 210

Key features of these books:

❏   Written in simple and lucid language

❏   Presented in step-by-step, easy-to-understand format with detailed explanations with appropriate images & screenshots, charts & tables

❏   Useful tips and notes given in every chapter as additional information

This book **"Comprehensive Computer Learning – Microsoft PowerPoint 2010"** has been written keeping in mind the needs of layman. MS Office & PowerPoint with its new look & real in its 2010 version is becoming more popular at offices & home and the book explains the basics of the same in some detail.

While every effort has been made to minimise printing and other errors, it may be possible that a few might have managed to escape the wakeful eyes. We would like to request the readers to bring these errors to our notice so that we can rectify the same in subsequent editions.

Comprehensive Computer Learning

Microsoft PowerPoint 2010

Bittu Kumar

V&S PUBLISHERS

Published by:

V&S PUBLISHERS

F-2/16, Ansari road, Daryaganj, New Delhi-110002
☎ 23240026, 23240027 • *Fax:* 011-23240028
Email: info@vspublishers.com • *Website:* www.vspublishers.com

Regional Office : Hyderabad

5-1-707/1, Brij Bhawan (Beside Central Bank of India Lane)
Bank Street, Koti, Hyderabad - 500 095
☎ 040-24737290
E-mail: vspublishershyd@gmail.com

Branch Office : Mumbai

Jaywant Industrial Estate, 1st Floor–108, Tardeo Road
Opposite Sobo Central Mall, Mumbai – 400 034
☎ 022-23510736
E-mail: vspublishersmum@gmail.com

Follow us on:

© Copyright: *V&S PUBLISHERS*
Edition 2018

Printed at Repro Knowledgecast Limited, Thane

Preface

This book is for the users of Microsoft PowerPoint 2010 who want to learn the program without wasting time and efforts. Look in this book to find out how you can get your work done better and faster. Here we will discuss basic and advanced concepts of MS PowerPoint.

What Makes this Book Different

You are holding in your hands a computer book designed to make mastering the MS PowerPoint as easy and comfortable as possible. Besides the fact that this book is easy to read, it's different from other books about Office. Read on to see why.

What do you need

❑ Latest Edition of Microsoft PowerPoint 2010

❑ Windows operating system: All people who have the Windows operating system installed on their computers are invited to read this book. It serves for people who have Windows 7, Windows Vista, Windows XP, and Windows NT.

❑ Basic Knowledge of English

What will you get

After a comprehensive reading of this book you will be able to do a variety of jobs. And you will notice that now you can do office-related works also.

– Bittu Kumar

Contents

Common Office Tools

Installing MS Office 2010

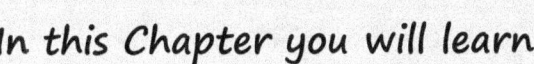

In this Chapter you will learn

- How to Install Microsoft-Office 2010 on your Computer.
- Step-by-step guide of installing Microsoft Office 2010 on your Computer.

The Most Important thing is installing the Microsoft Office on your Systems First. You can do it by purchasing a genuine copy of Microsoft Office from nearest software outlet, or simply download it from the Microsoft's official website. Here we are discussing setup instructions for Microsoft Office Professional Plus 2010.

After buying CD/Downloading files, follow these Instructions:

✓ Go to the File directory where the Microsoft office setup is.

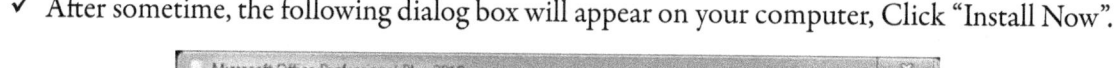

✓ Now click on Setup.exe and click on yes (In the case you are using Windows 7 or Vista).

✓ After sometime, the following dialog box will appear on your computer, Click "Install Now".

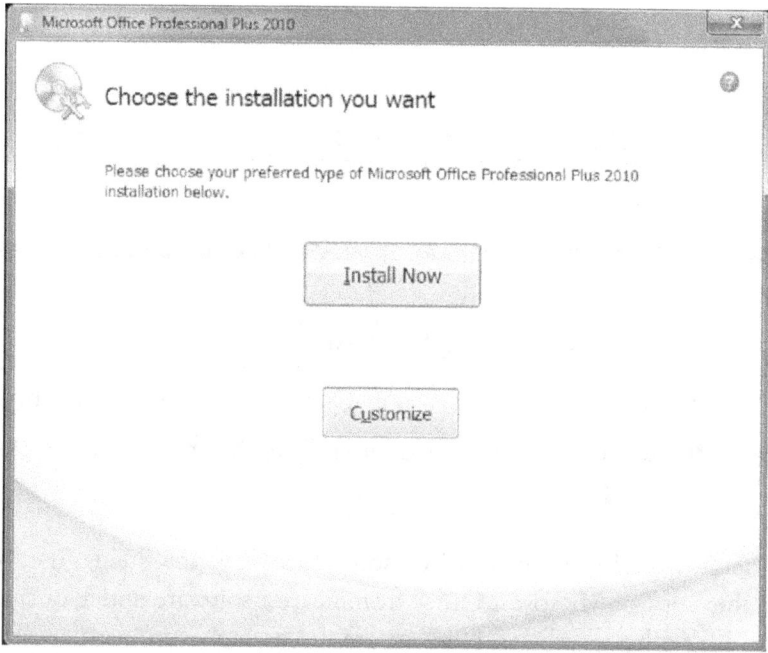

✓ The following box will appear on clicking "Install Now", wait for a few minutes and let Microsoft office 2011 be installed on your system.

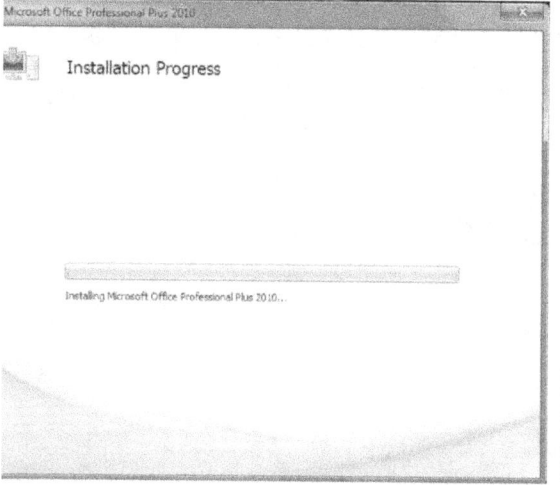 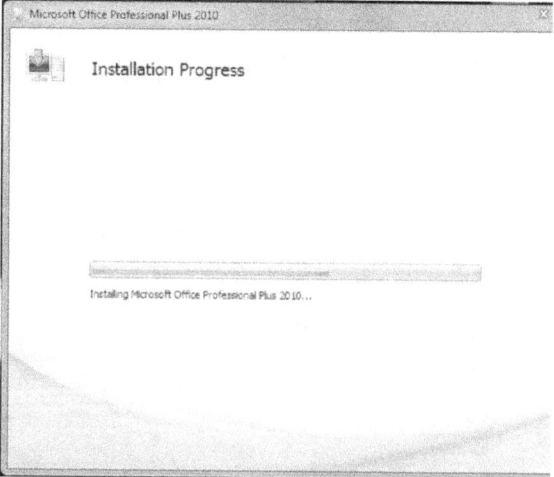

✓ Then Click "Close" and Cheers; you are done!

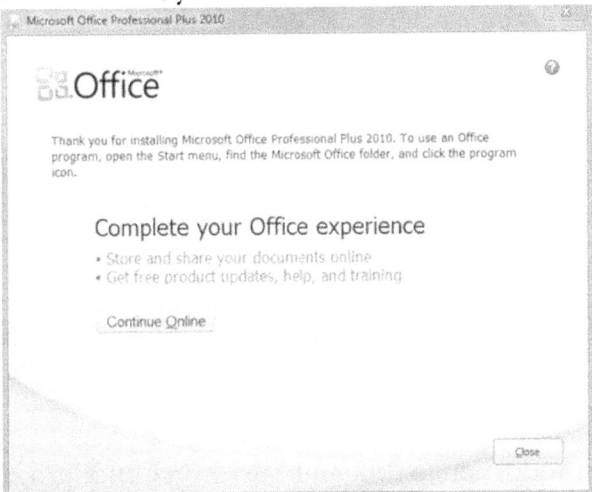

Now you have successfully Installed Microsoft office 2010 on your Computer. Now we shall begin Microsoft Office 2010 Basic Course

Points to Remember

☞ *Always use genuine software from Microsoft. Pirated software may contain Viruses & other Malwares.*

☞ *Your Serial-Key is personal to you; don't share it with anyone before installing and activating the Product.*

☞ *Never download the Microsoft Product from any other website other than Microsoft. You can try beta versions before you buy.*

Introduction to MS Office

In this chapter you will learn

- Introduction to different Microsoft Office programs
- Basic Information on the Graphical-User Interference
- Using different tabs in office Programs
- Creating, Saving & Editing your work
- Saving File in the earlier versions of Microsoft Office
- Encrypting the documents

Office 2010, sometimes called the Microsoft Office Suite, is a collection of computer programs. Why is it called Office? I think, because the people who developed it wanted to make software for completing tasks that need doing in a typical office. When you hear someone talk about "Office" or the "Office Software," they're talking about several different programs:

❑ **Word:** A word processor for writing letters, reports, and so on. A Word file is called a document.

❑ **Outlook:** A personal information manager, scheduler, and e-mailer.

❑ **PowerPoint:** A means of creating slide presentations to give in front of audiences. A PowerPoint file is called a presentation, or sometimes a slide show.

❑ **Excel:** A Part of office for performing numerical analyses. An Excel file is called a workbook.

❑ **Access:** A database management program.

❑ **Publisher:** A means of creating desktop-publishing files — pamphlets, notices, newsletters, and even books!

If you're new to Office, don't study so many different computer programs. The programs have much in common. You find the same commands throughout Office. For example, the method of choosing fonts is the same in Word, Outlook, PowerPoint, Excel, Access, and Publisher. Creating diagrams and charts works the same way in Word, PowerPoint, and Excel.

Starting an Office Program

Unless you start an Office program, you can't create a document, construct a worksheet, or make a database. Learn how you can do that.

✓ Click the Start button, choose All Programs → Microsoft Office, and then choose the program's name on the submenu.

User Interface in Microsoft Office

Interface, also called the user interface, is a computer term that describes how a software program presents itself to the people who use it.

Introduction to the GUI

❑ File tab

In the upper-left corner of the window is the File tab, Go to the File tab to find commands for creating, opening, and saving files, as well as doing other file-management tasks. Notice

the Options command. You can choose Options to open the Options dialog box and tell the program you are working in how you want it to work.

The Ribbon and its tabs

Across the top of the screen is the Ribbon, an assortment of different tabs; click a tab to undertake a task. For example, click the Home tab to format text; click the Insert tab to insert a table or chart.

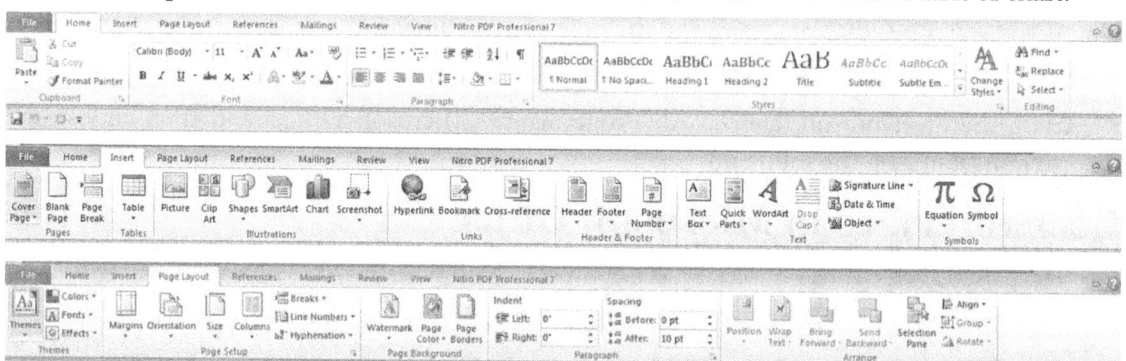

Your first step when you start a new task is to click a tab on the Ribbon. Knowing which tab to click takes a while, but the names of tabs — Home, Insert, View, and so on — hint as to which commands you find while you visit a tab.

To make the Ribbon disappear and get more room to view items on-screen, click the Minimize the Ribbon button (or press Ctrl+F1). This button is located on the right side of the Ribbon, to the left of the Help button. You can also right-click the Ribbon and choose Minimize the Ribbon on the shortcut menu, or double-click a tab on the Ribbon. To see the Ribbon again, click the Minimize the Ribbon button, press Ctrl+F1, double-click a Ribbon tab or right-click a tab name or the Quick Access toolbar and deselect Minimize the Ribbon on the shortcut menu. While the Ribbon is minimized, you can click a tab name to display a tab.

The Description of a tab

Groups

Commands on each tab are organized into groups. The names of these groups appear below the buttons and galleries on tabs. For example, the Home tab in Word is organized into several groups, including the Clipboard, Font, Paragraph, Styles.

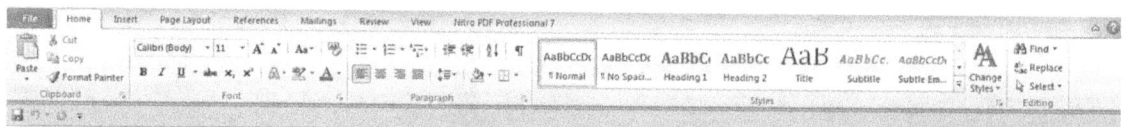

Groups do the following:

❑ Groups tell you what the buttons and galleries above their names are used for. On the Home tab in Word, for example, the buttons in the Font group are for formatting text. Read group names to help find the command you need.

❑ Many groups have a group button that you can click to open a dialog box or task pane (officially, Microsoft calls these little buttons dialog launcher).

Buttons

Go to any tab and you find buttons of all shapes and sizes. Square buttons and rectangular buttons; big and small buttons, buttons with labels and buttons without labels. Is there any rhyme or reason to these button shapes and sizes? No, there isn't. What matters isn't a button's shape or size, but whether a down-pointingarrow appears on its face:

❑ A button with an arrow: Click a button with an arrow and you get a drop-down list with options you can select.

❑ A button without an arrow: Click a button without an arrow and you complete an action of some kind.

❑ A hybrid button with an arrow: Some buttons serve a dual purpose as a button and a drop-down list. By clicking the symbol on the top half of the button, you complete an action; by clicking the arrow on the bottom half of the button, you open a drop-down list. On the Home tab, for example, clicking the top half of the Paste button pastes what is on the Clipboard into your file, but clicking the bottom half of the button opens a drop-down list with Paste options.

Keyboard Shortcuts

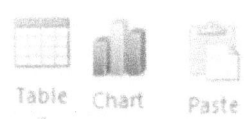

People who like to give commands by pressing keyboard shortcuts may well ask, "Is there keyboard shortcuts in Office?" The answer is: Yes, Office has shortcuts. For example, you can press Ctrl+B to boldface text and Ctrl+U tounderline text. Office offers Alt+key shortcuts as well.

Saving Your Files

Soon after you create a file, be sure to save it. And save your file from time to time while you work on it as well. Until you save your work, it rests in the computer's electronic memory (**Random Access Memory**), a precarious location. If a power outage occurs, you may lose all the work you did since the last time you saved your file. Make it a habit to save files every five Minutes or so or when you are doing an important task. Choose the folder where you want to save a file, declare

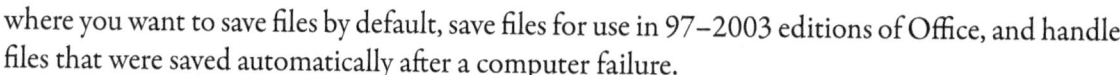

where you want to save files by default, save files for use in 97–2003 editions of Office, and handle files that were saved automatically after a computer failure.

To save a file:

✓ Click the Save button (you find it on the Quick Access toolbar).

✓ Press Ctrl+S.

✓ Go to the File tab and choose Save.

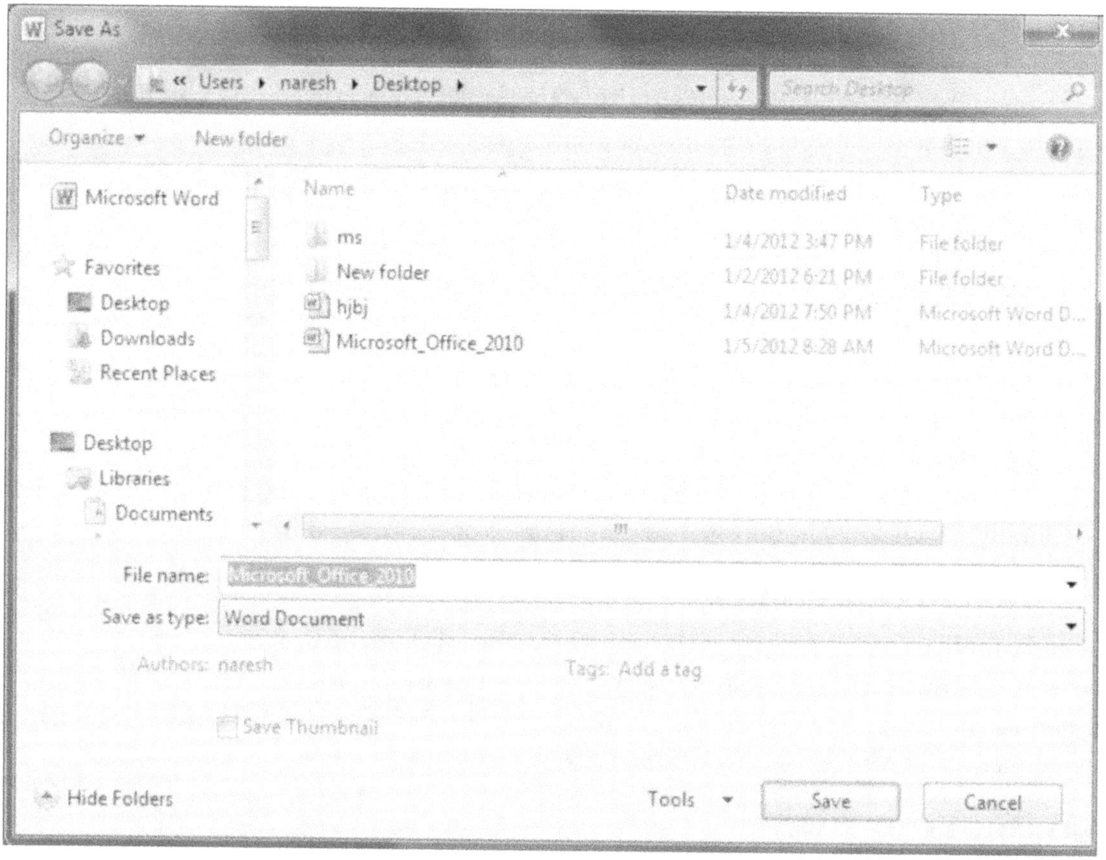

Where you like to save files

To direct Office to the folder you like best and make it appear first in the Save As and Open dialog boxes, follow these steps:

✓ In Word, Excel, PowerPoint, or Access, go to the File tab and choose Options.

You see the Options dialog box.

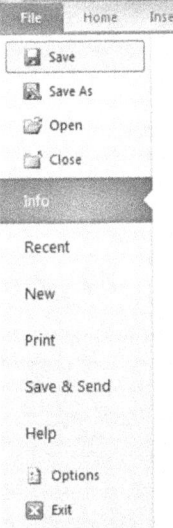

✓ In Word, Excel, and PowerPoint, select the Save category; in Access, select the General category.

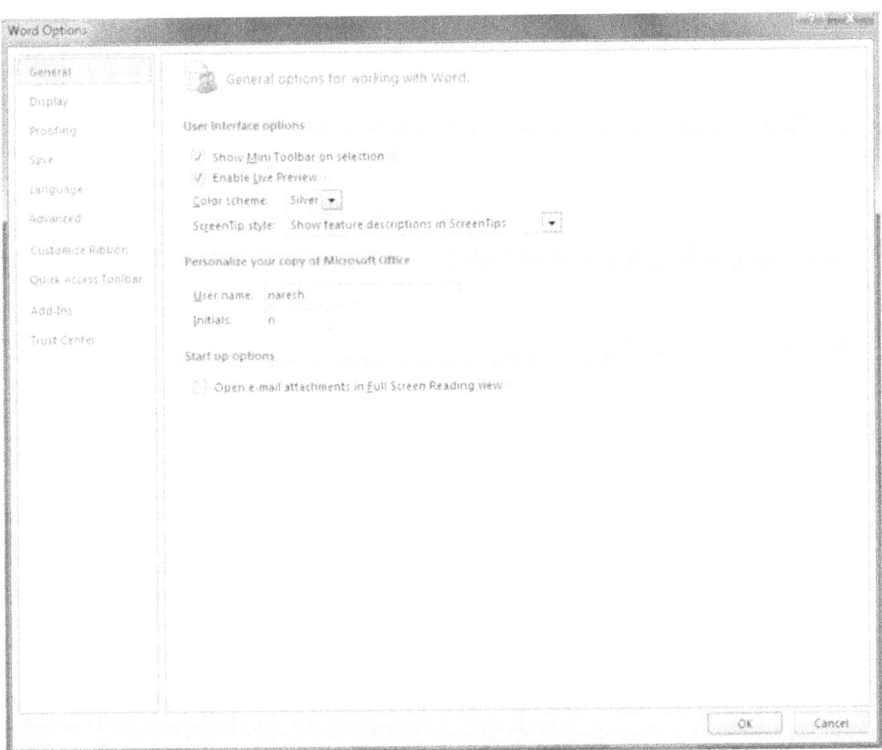

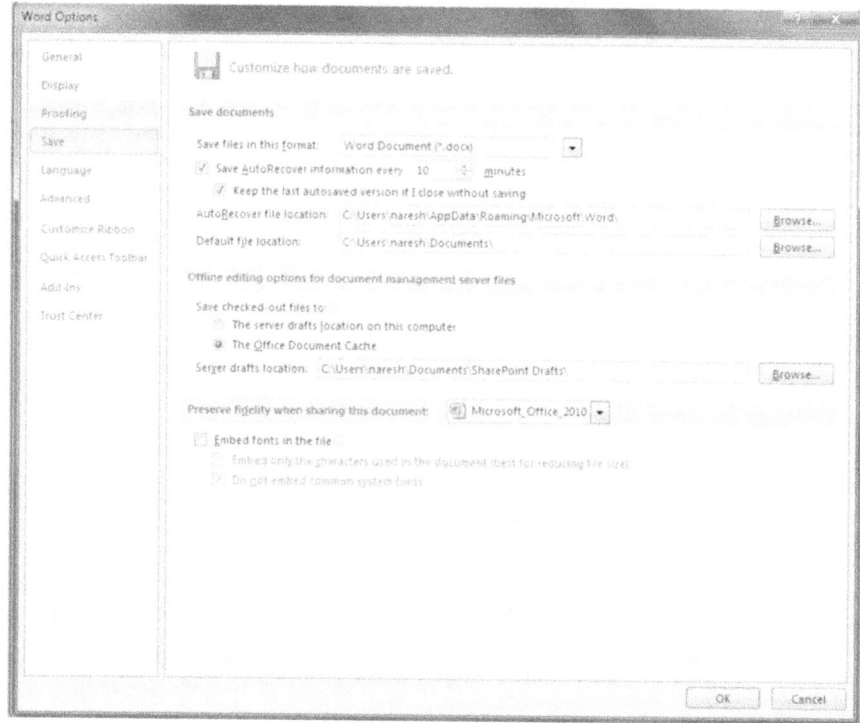

Saving a file in word

Saving files for use in earlier versions of an Office program

Before you pass along a file to a user who has Office 2003, XP, 2000, or 97, save your document in these versions so that the other person can open it. People with versions of Office prior to version 2010 and 2007 cannot open your Office files unless you save your files for earlier versions of Office.

Program	2010, 2007	97–2003
Access	.accdb	.mlb
Excel	.xlsx	.xls
PowerPoint	.pptx	.ppt
Publisher	.pub	.pub
Word	.docx	.doc

Saving a file for use in Office 97–2003

Follow these steps to save a file so that someone with Office 97, 2000, XP, or2003 can open it:

✓ Go to the File tab.

✓ Choose Save & Send.

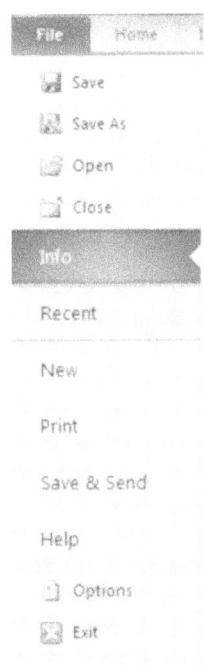

✓ You see the Share window.

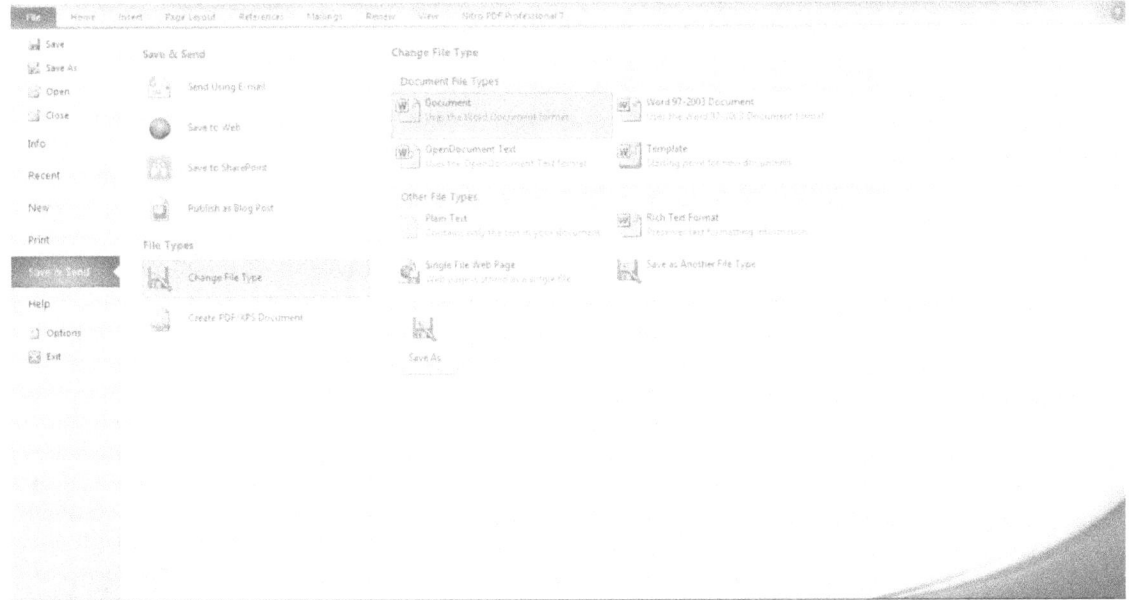

✓ Under File Types, choose Change File Type and then choose 97–2003 option for saving files. The Save As dialog box opens.

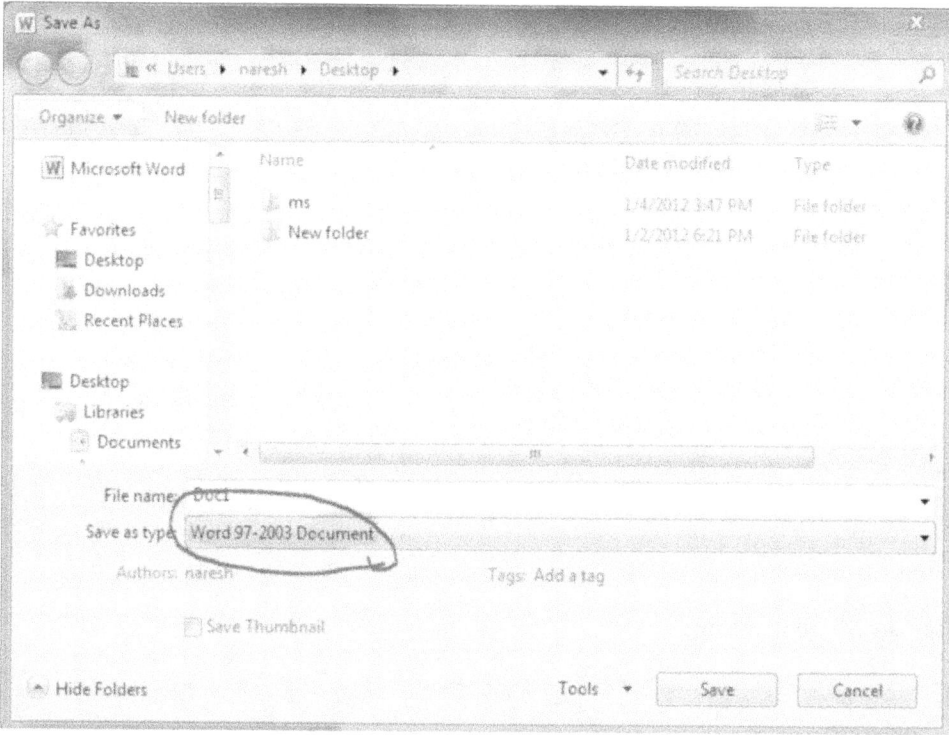

✓ Enter a new name for the file, if necessary.

✓ Click the Save button.

Saving Auto Recovery information

To insure against data loss due to computer and power failures, Office saves files on its own every ten minutes. These files are saved in an Auto Recovery file. You can try to recover some of the work you lost by getting it from the Auto Recovery file.

Convert Earlier Version of word to 2010

Convert

Compatibility Mode

Some new features are disabled to prevent problems when working with previous versions of Office. Converting this file will enable these features, but may result in layout changes.

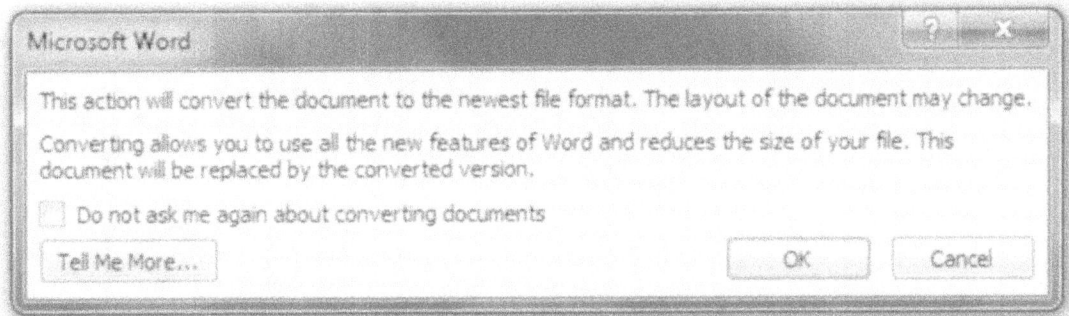

Go to File → Convert→ Click "Okay"

The Save As and Open Dialog Boxes

The Open dialog box and Save As dialog box offer a bunch of different ways to locate a file you want to open or locate the folder where you want to save a file.

Searching for files in a folder: Use the Search box to search for subfolders and files in the folder you is currently viewing. After you type the first few letters of a file name or subfolder, you see only the names of items that start with the letters you typed. To see all the files and subfolders again, click the Close button (the X) in the Search box.

Changing views: Display folder contents differently by choosing a view on the Views drop-down list (in Windows 7, look for the View arrow in the upper-right corner of the dialog box). In Details view, you see how large files are and when they were last edited.

Creating a new folder: Click the New Folder button to create a new subfolder for storing files. Select the folder that your new folder will be subordinate to and click the New Folder button. Then type a name forthe saved file.

Navigate to different folders: Click the Folders bar (in the lower-left corner of the dialog box) to open the Navigation pane and look for folders or presentations on a different drive, network location, or folder on your computer.

Opening a file

✓ On the File tab, choose Open (or press Ctrl+O).

✓ Locate and select the file you want to open.

✓ Click the Open button.

✓ Your file opens. You can also double-click a filename to open a file.

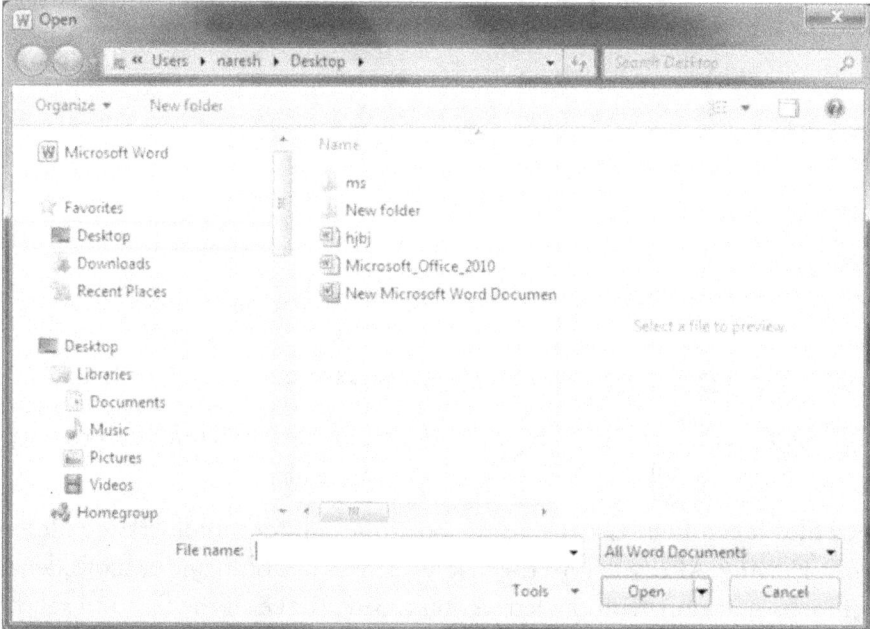

✓ If you have recently accessed the file you can use recent button in file tab.

File Properties

Properties are a means of describing a file. If you manage more files, you owe it to yourself to record properties. You can use them later to identify files.

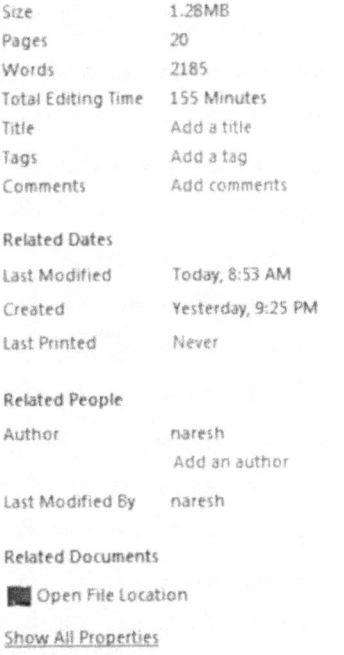

Permissions

Anyone can open, copy, and change any part of this document.

Locking a File with a Password

To read property descriptions, go to the File tab and examine the Information window. Property descriptions are found on the right side of the window.

Follow these steps to clamp a password on a file, such that others need apassword to open and perhaps also edit it:

✓ Go to the File tab.

✓ In the Information window, click the Protect Document (or Workbook) button, and choose Encrypt with Password on the drop-down list.

✓ Enter a password in the Password text box and click OK.

Others will need the password you enter to open the file. They have to enter the password. Passwords are case-sensitive. In other words, you have to enter the correct combination of upper- and lowercase letters to successfully enter the

Properties ▾

Size	1.28MB
Pages	20
Words	2185
Total Editing Time	155 Minutes
Title	Add a title
Tags	Add a tag
Comments	Add comments

Related Dates

Last Modified	Today, 8:53 AM
Created	Yesterday, 9:25 PM
Last Printed	Never

Related People

Author	naresh
	Add an author
Last Modified By	naresh

Related Documents

Open File Location

Show All Properties

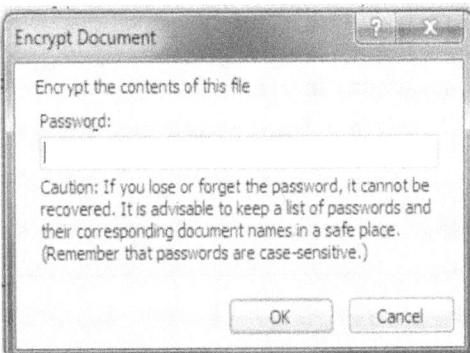

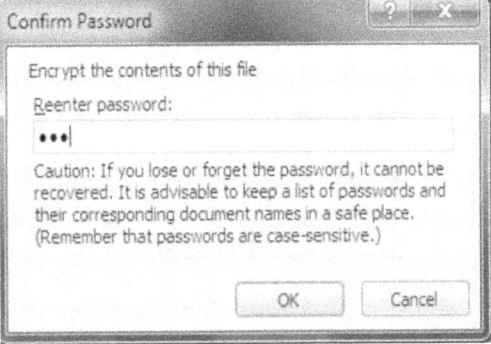

password. If the password is Apple (with an uppercase A), mentoring apple (with a lowercase a) is deemed the wrong passwordand doesn't open the file.

✓ In the Confirm Password dialog box, enter the password again.

✓ Click OK.

The Information window informs you that a password is required to open the file.

Removing Password

Follow these steps to remove a password from a file:

✓ Open the file that needs its password removed.

✓ Go to the File tab and in the Information window, click the Protect Document button, and choose Encrypt with Password.

✓ Delete the password and click OK.

Points to Remember

☞ Always save your files with custom names, so that you can easily index your files. Using default names for multiple files will waste your time in finding out which file you need to edit once you have closed the file.

☞ To keep the file size minimum save the file in 2010 format, it will save your disk space.

☞ Always keep your files in the Custom directory other than Primary Hard disk (This will help in you safeguarding your files against any system faliures). In other words never save your important files in C: / (C:/ here stands for primary directory, the primary directory may vary for different users)

☞ The Passwords are Case Sensitive; there is no way to recover forgotten passwords so confirm twice that you can remember it.

☞ Never use any foreign software for extracting/removing the password, it will harm your computer.

☞ If you are running your Computer in frequent power-cut environment, please save your file frequently to save your hard work in editing the file.

☞ Use Keyboard shortcuts to save your time.

- ☞ Use variety of names for saving your file, for example if you write essay on Independence day, your system will give your document a default name of "New Microsoft word Document X.docx (X~ some number), you can save your file as "Independence day.docx" to remember the file if you need further editing after quitting.
- ☞ Never save your file at insecure places (Web directory, etc.) where a hacker can easily access it.
- ☞ Make sure that you have an updated Anti-Malware protection enabled on your system.
- ☞ Please scan the documents with your Anti-Malware software before opening them. Most probably the Files downloaded from Internet contains some spywares, adware, Trojan horses & some other harmful programs.
- ☞ Never edit any document having other extensions than discussed in the chapter, it can corrupt the file. (For example if you open .pdf files with MS Word & Edit it, this will corrupt its contents.)

Formatting Text

In this chapter you will learn

- Ways to select different elements of the file or document
- Formatting font styles and other Elements
- Changing the size, colour, opacity of the elements in the file or document
- Using Symbols & formulae in the file or document
- Finding and replacing data in the file or document
- Creating Links to files & websites

Selecting text

Before you can perform any activity to any text you have to select it.

To Select	Do This
A word	Double-click the word.
A few words	Drag over the words.
A paragraph	Triple-click inside the paragraph
A block of text	Click the start of the text, hold down the Shift key, and click the end of the text. In Word you can also click the start of the text, press F8, and click at the end of the text.
All text	Press Ctrl+A.

Moving and Copying text

✓ **Dragging and Dropping:** Move the mouse over the text and then click and drag the text to a new location. Drag means to hold down the mouse button while you move the pointer on-screen. If you want to copy rather than move the text, hold down the Ctrl key while you drag.

✓ **Dragging and Dropping with the right mouse button**: Drag the text while holding down the right, not the left, mouse button. After you release the right mouse button, a shortcut menu appears with Move Here and Copy Here options. Choose an option to move or copy the text.

✓ **Using the Clipboard**: Move or copy the text to the Clipboard by clicking the Cut or Copy button, pressing Ctrl+X or Ctrl+C, or right-clicking and choosing Cut or Copy on the shortcut menu. The text is moved or copied to an electronic holding tank called the Clipboard. Paste the text by clicking the Paste button, pressing Ctrl+V, or right-clicking and choosing Paste. You can find the Paste, Cut, and Copy buttons on the Hometab.

Deleting text

To delete a bunch of text, select the text you want to delete and press the Delete key.

Changing the Look of Text

What text looks like is determined by its font, the size of the letters, the colour of the letters, and whether text effects or font styles such as italic or boldface are in the text. The text's appearance really matters in Word, PowerPoint, and Publisher because files you create in those programs are meant to be read by all and sundry. Even in Excel, Access, and Outlook messages, font choices matter because the choices you make determine whether your work is easy to read and understand.

A font is a collection of letters, numbers, and symbols in a particular typeface, including all italic and boldface variations of the letters, numbers, and symbols.

Choosing fonts for text

✓ **Mini-toolbar:** Move the pointer over the selected text. You see the mini toolbar. Move the pointer over this toolbar and choose a font in the Font drop-down list.

✓ **Shortcut menu:** Right-click the selected text and choose a new font on the shortcut menu.

✓ **Font drop-down list:** On the Home tab, open the Font drop-down list and choose a font.

✓ **Font dialog box:** On the Home tab, click the Font group button. You see the Font dialog box. select a font and click OK.

Changing the font size of text

✓ Font size is measured in points; a point is 1/72 of an inch.

✓ **Mini-toolbar:** Move the pointer over the text, and when you see the mini toolbar, move the pointer over the toolbar and choose a font size on the Font.

✓ **Shortcut menu:** Right-click the text and choose a new font size on the shortcut menu.

✓ **Font Size drop-down list:** On the Home tab, open the Font Size dropdown list and choose a font. You can live-preview font sizes this way.

✓ **Font dialog box:** On the Home tab, click the Font group button, and in the Font dialog box, choose a font size and click OK.

✓ **Increase Font Size and Decrease Font Size buttons:** Click these buttons (or press Ctrl+] or Ctrl+[) to increase or decrease the point size by the next interval on the Font Size drop-down list.

Applying font styles to text

❑ **Regular:** This style is just Office's way of denoting an absence of any font style.

❑ **Italic:** You can also italicize titles to make them a little more elegant. (Ctrl+I)

❑ **Bold:** Bold text calls attention to itself. (Ctrl+B)

❑ **Underline:** Underlined text also calls attention to itself, but use underlining sparingly. Later in this chapter, "Underlining text" discusses all the ways to underline text.

❑ **Strikethrough and double strikethrough:** By convention, strikethrough is used to show where passages are struck from a contract or other important document.

❑ **Subscript:** A subscripted letter is lowered in the text. In the chemical formula below, the 2 is lowered to show that two atoms of hydrogen are needed along with one atom of oxygen to form a molecule of water: H_2O. (Press Ctrl+=.)

❑ **Superscript:** A superscripted letter or number is one that is raised in the text. Superscript is used in mathematical and scientific formulas, in ordinal numbers (1st, 2nd , 3rd), and to mark footnotes. In the theory of relativity, the 2 is superscripted: $E = mc^2$. (Press Ctrl+Shift+plus sign.)

Changing the colour of text

✓ On the mini-toolbar, open the drop-down list on the Font Colour button and choose a colour.

✓ Right-click, open the drop-down list on the Font Colour button, and choose a colour on the shortcut menu.

✓ On the Home tab, open the drop-down list on the Font Colour button and choose a colour.

✓ On the Home tab, click the Font group button to open the Font dialog box, open the Font Colour drop-down list, and choose a colour. The Font Colour drop-down list offers theme colours and standard colours. You are well advised to choose a theme colour. These colours are deemed theme colours because they jive with the theme you choose for your file.

Changing Case

To change case in Word and PowerPoint, all you have to do is select the text, go to the Home tab, click the Change Case button, and choose an option on the drop-down list:

❏ **Sentence case:** Renders the letters in sentence case.

❏ **lowercase:** Makes all the letters lowercase.

❏ **UPPERCASE:** Renders all the letters as capital letters.

❏ **Capitalize Each Word:** Capitalizes the first letter of each word. If you choose this option for a title or heading, go into the title and lower case the first letter of articles (the, a, an), coordinate conjunctions (and, or, for, nor), and prepositions unless they're the first or last word in the title.

❏ **TOGGLE CASE:** Choose this option if you accidentally enter letters with the Caps Lock key pressed.

Entering Symbols and Foreign Characters

✓ On the Insert tab, click the Symbol button. (You may have to click the Symbols button first, depending on the size of your screen)

✓ If you're looking to insert a symbol, not a foreign character, choose Webdings or Wingdings 1, 2, or 3 in the Font drop-down list.

✓ Webdings and Wingdings fonts offer all kinds of weird and wacky symbols.

✓ Select a symbol or foreign character.

✓ Click the Insert button to enter the symbol and then click Close to close the dialog box.

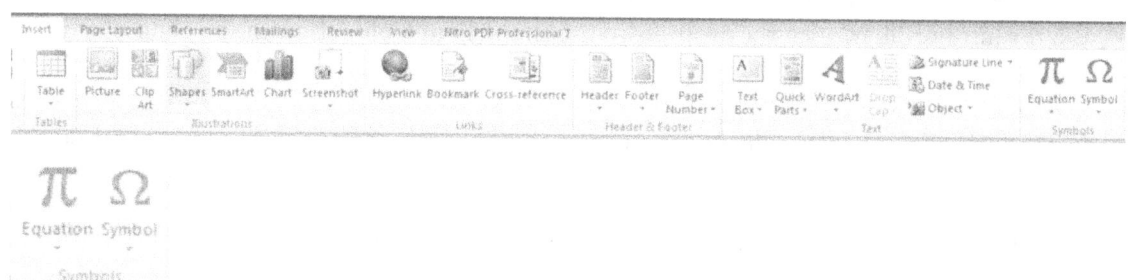

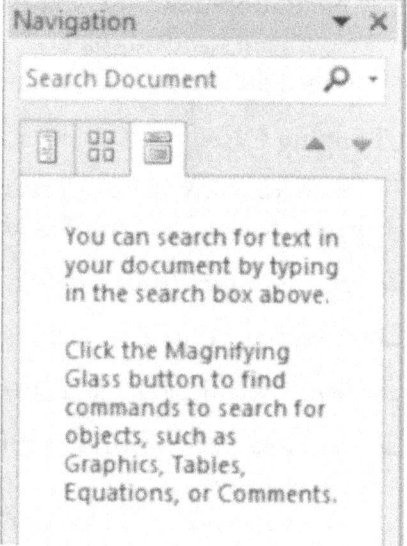

Finding and Replacing Text

✓ Press Ctrl+F or go to the Home tab and click the Find button. (In Excel, click the Find & Select button and choose Find on the dropdown list.)

✓ Enter the word or phrase in the Find What or Search Documenttext box.

After you enter the word or phrase in Word, the Navigation pane lists each instance of the term you're looking for and the term is highlighted in your document wherever it is found. You can click an instance of the search term in the Navigation pane to scroll to a location in your document where the search term is located. You can also remove the word using replace.

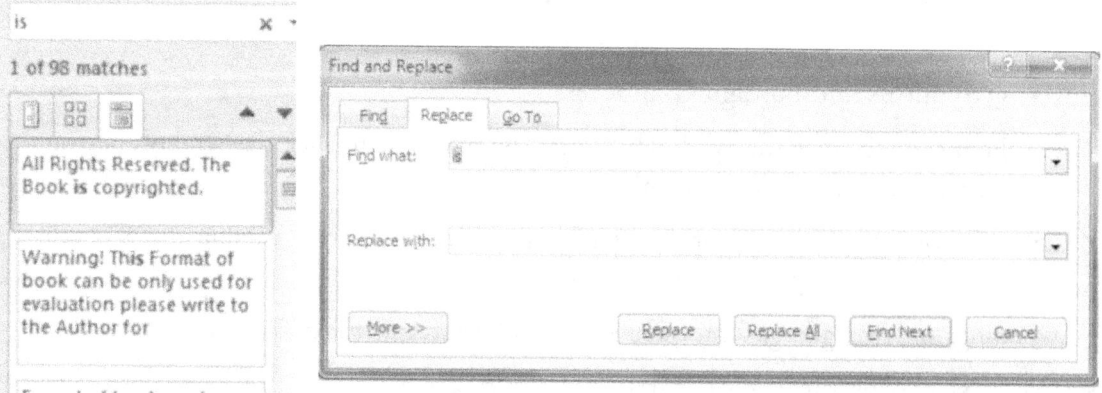

Finding and Replacing text

Creating Hyperlinks

A hyperlink is an electronic shortcut from one place to another. Clicking hyperlinks on the Internet takes you to different web pages or different places on the same web page. In the Office programs, you can use hyperlinks to connect readers to your favourite web pages or to a different page, slide, or file.

Select the text or object that will form the hyperlink.

For example, select a line of text or phrase if you want viewers to be able to click it to go to a web page.

✓ On the Insert tab, click the Hyperlink button (or press Ctrl+K). Depending on the size of your screen, you may have to click the Links button before you can get to the Hyperlink button. You can also open this dialog box by right-clicking an object or text and choosing Hyperlink on the shortcut menu

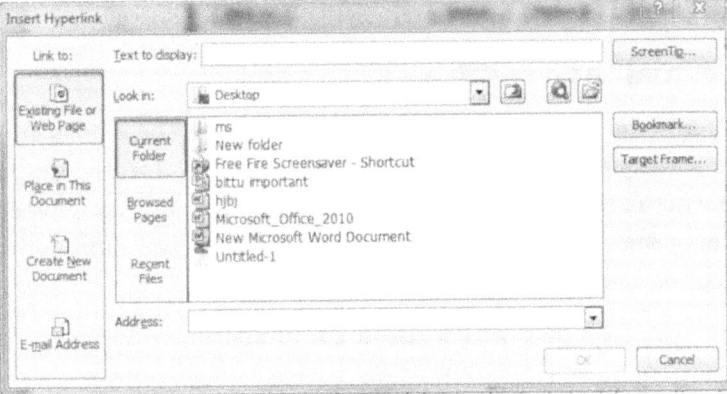

Creating Hyperlink

✓ **Click Browse the Web button:** Your web browser opens after you click this button. Go to the web page you want to link to and return to your program. The web page's address appears in the Address text box.

✓ **Click Browsed Pages:** The dialog box lists web pages you recently visited after you click this button, Type (or copy) a web page address into the Address text box: Enter the address of the web page. You can right-click the text box and choose Paste to copy a web page address into the text box.

✓ Click the ScreenTip button, enter a ScreenTip in the Set HyperlinkScreenTip dialog box, and click OK.

✓ Click OK in the Insert Hyperlink dialog box.

Creating a hyperlink to another place in your file

Follow these steps to create a hyperlink to another place in your file:

✓ Select the text or object that will form the hyperlink.

✓ On the Insert tab, click the Hyperlink button (or press Ctrl+K). You see the Insert Hyperlink dialog box. Another way to open this dialog box is to right-click and choose Hyperlink in the shortcut menu.

✓ Under Link To, select Place in This Document. What you see in the dialog box depends on which program you're working in.

✓ Select the target of the hyperlink. Click the ScreenTip button.

✓ You see the Set Hyperlink ScreenTip dialog box.

✓ Enter a ScreenTip and click OK. When viewers move their pointers over the link, they see the words you enter. Enter a description of where the hyperlink takes you.

Creating an e-mail hyperlink

✓ An e-mail hyperlink is one that opens an e-mail program. These links are sometimes found on web pages so that anyone visiting a web page can conveniently send an e-mail message to the person who manages the web page. When you click an e-mail hyperlink, your default e-mail program opens. And If the person who set up the link was thorough about it, the e-mail message is already addressed and given a subject line.

✓ Select the words or object that will constitute the link.

✓ On the Insert tab, click the Hyperlink button (or press Ctrl+K). The Insert Hyperlink dialog box appears.

✓ Under Link To, click E-Mail Address. Text boxes appear for entering an e-mail address and a subject message.

✓ Enter your e-mail address and a subject for the messages that others will send you. Office inserts the word mail to: before your e-mail address as you enter it.

✓ Click OK.

Repairing and removing hyperlinks

✓ **Repairing a link:** Select a target in your file or a web page and click OK.

✓ **Removing a link:** Click the Remove Link button. You can also remove a hyperlink by right-clicking the link and choosing Remove.

Points to Remember

☞ Practice selecting skills at your best before creating custom documents
☞ While hyperlinking, double check that the directory exits
☞ While hyperlinking make sure that you don't hyperlink your files present at sensitive locations

4th Chapter

Get more from Office

In this chapter you will learn

- Tracking changes to a document or file
- Accessibility options in Microsoft office 2010
- Using language Tools

Undoing and Repeating Commands

Undo allows you to reverse actions you regret doing, and the Repeat repeats a previous action without you have to choose the same commands all over again. All is not lost if you make a big blunder because Office has a marvelous little tool called the Undo command. This command "Remembers" your previous editorial and formatting changes. As long as you catch your error in time, you can undo your mistake.

✓ Click the Undo button on the Quick Access toolbar (or press Ctrl+Z) to undo your most recent change. If you made your error and went on to do something else before you caught it, open the drop-down list on the Undo button.

✓ Click Redo to redo the change.

Zooming

You can find these controls in the lower-right corner of the window and on the View tab

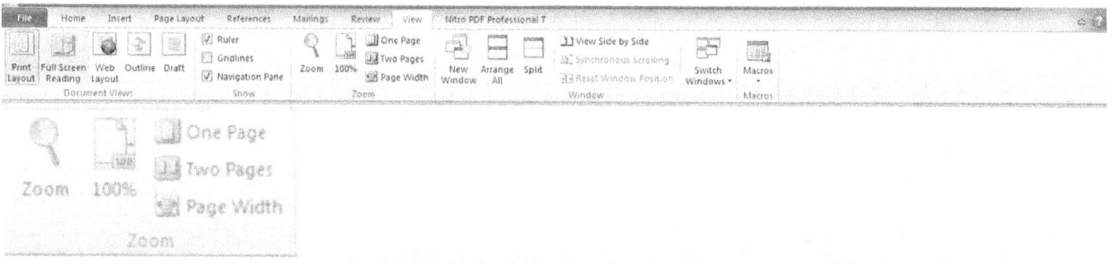

- **Zoom dialog box:** Click the Zoom button on the View tab or the Zoom box (the % listing) to display the Zoom dialog box; you can select an option button or enter a Percent measurement.

- **Zoom button:** Click the Zoom In or Zoom Out button on the Zoom slider to zoom in or out in 10-percent increments.

- **Zoom slider:** Drag the Zoom slider left to shrink or right to enlarge what is on your screen.

- **Mouse wheel:** If your mouse has a wheel, you can hold down the Ctrl key and spin the wheel to quickly zoom in or out.

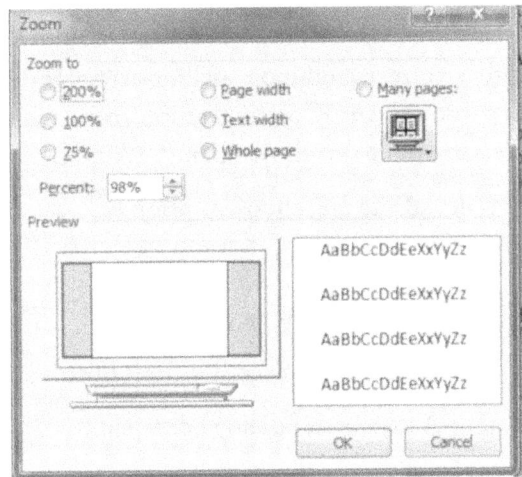

Zooming text

Viewing a File through more than One Window

- **New Window:** Opens another window on your file, so that you can view two places simultaneously in the same file. To go back and forth between windows, click a taskbar button or click the Switch Windows button and choose a window name on the drop-down list. Click window's Close button when you're finished looking at it.

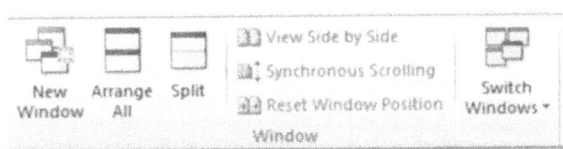

Viewing a file through more than one window

- **Arrange All:** Arranges open windows side by side on-screen.

- **Switch Windows:** Opens a drop-down list with open windows so that you can travel between windows.

- **View Side by Side:** Displays files side by side so that you can compare and contrast them.

- **Synchronous Scrolling:** Permits you to scroll two files at the same rate so that you can proofread one against the other. To use this command, start by clicking the View Side by Side button. After you click the Synchronous Scrolling button, click the Reset Window Position button so both files are displayed at the same size on-screen.

- **Reset Window Position:** Makes files being shown side by side the same size on-screen to make them easier to compare.

Opening AutoCorrect dialog box

Office corrects common spelling errors and turns punctuation mark combinations into symbols as part of its AutoCorrect feature. To see which typos are corrected and which punctuation marks are turned into symbols, open the AutoCorrect dialog box by following these steps:

- ✓ On the File tab, choose Options.
- ✓ You see the Options dialog box.
- ✓ Go to the Proofing category.
- ✓ Click the AutoCorrect Options button.
- ✓ The AutoCorrect dialog box opens.
- ✓ Click the AutoCorrect tab.
- ✓ AutoCorrect tab lists words that are corrected automatically. Scroll down the Replace list and have a look around. Go ahead and make yourself at home.

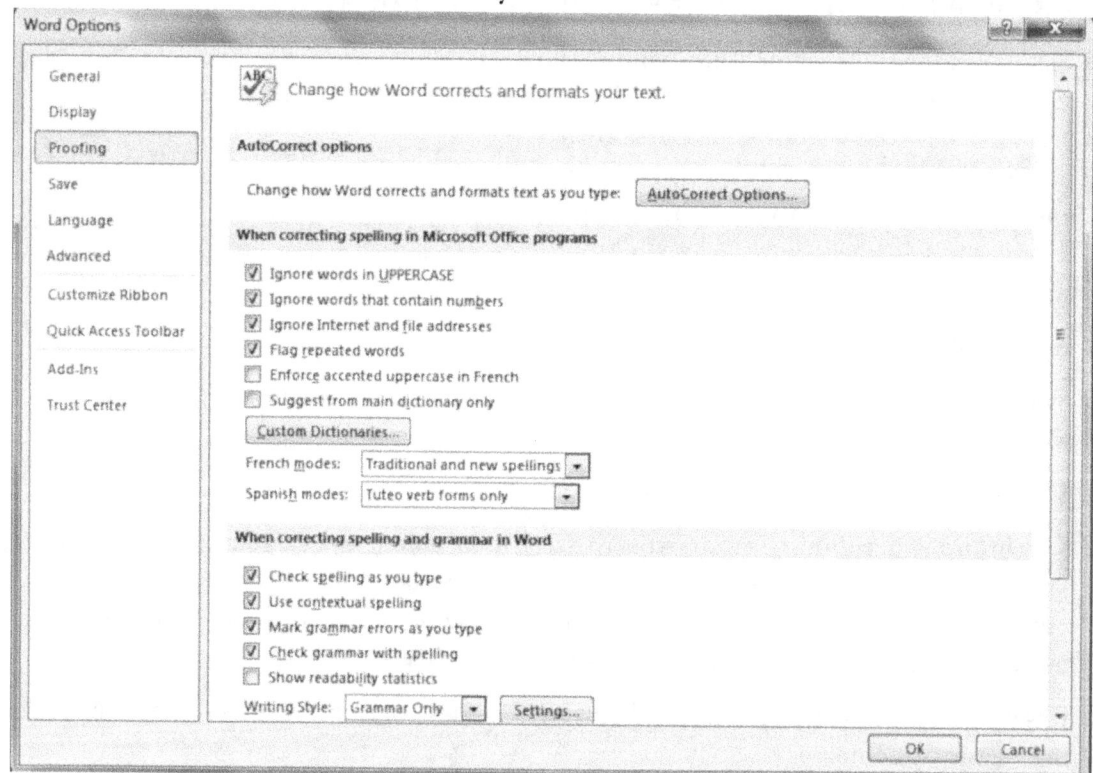

Auto correct dialog box

AutoCorrect: English (U.S.)

AutoFormat | Actions
AutoCorrect | Math AutoCorrect | AutoFormat As You Type

☑ Show AutoCorrect Options buttons

☑ Correct TWo INitial CApitals   Exceptions...
☑ Capitalize first letter of sentences
☑ Capitalize first letter of table cells
☑ Capitalize names of days
☑ Correct accidental usage of cAPS LOCK key

☑ Replace text as you type
Replace: With: ⦿ Plain text   ○ Formatted text

(c)	©
(e)	€
(r)	®
(tm)	™
...	...
:(	☺

☑ Automatically use suggestions from the spelling checker

OK   Cancel

Checking for Grammatical Errors in Word

You can do your best to repair grammatical errors in Word documents by getting the assistance of the grammar checker. The grammar checker identifies grammatical errors, explains what the errors are, and gives you the opportunity to correct the errors. Sentences in which grammatical errors appear are underlined in blue in your document. Meanwhile, the grammatical errors themselves appear in bright blue in the box at the top of the Spelling and Grammar dialog box (alongwith spelling errors, which are red). When Word encounters an error, take one of these actions to correct it:

✓ Select a correction in the Suggestions box and click the Change button.

✓ Delete the grammatical error or rephrase the sentence in the top of the dialog box, enter a correction, and click the Change button.

✓ Click outside the Spelling and Grammar dialog box, correct the grammatical error in your document, and then click the Resume button (you find it where the Ignore Once button used to be).
Click one of the Ignore buttons to let what Word thinks is a grammatical error stand.

Researching a Topic inside an Office Program

Thanks to the Research task pane, your desk needn't be as crowded as before. The Research task pane offers dictionaries, foreign language dictionaries, a thesaurus, language translators, and encyclopedias, as well as Internet searching, all available from inside the Office programs.

Finding the Right Word with the Thesaurus

To search for a good synonym, click the word in question and open the thesaurus on the Research task pane with one of these techniques:

✓ Press Shift+F7.

✓ Right-click the word and choose Synonym ➜ Thesaurus.

✓ Go to the Review tab and click the Thesaurus button.

The Research task pane opens. It offers a list of synonyms and sometimes includes an antonym or two at the bottom. Now you're getting somewhere:

❏ **Choosing a synonym:** Move the pointer over the synonym you want, open its drop-down list, and choose Insert.

❏ **Finding a synonym for a synonym:** If a synonym intrigues you, click it. The task pane displays a new list of synonyms.

❏ **Searching for antonyms:** If you can't think of the right word, type its antonym in the Search For box and then look for an "antonym of an antonym" in the Research task pane.

❏ **Revisit a word list:** Click the Back button as many times as necessary. If you go back too far, you can always click its companion Forward button.

Telling Office which languages you will use

Follow these steps to inform Word, PowerPoint, Publisher, and Outlook that you will use a language or languages besides English in your files:

✓ On the Review tab, click the Language button and choose Language Preferences. The Options dialog box opens to the Language category.

Language

✓ Open the Add Additional Editing Languages drop-down list, select a language, and click the Add button to make that language a part of your presentations, documents, and messages.

✓ Click OK.

Marking text as foreign language text

The next step is to tell Office where in your file you're using a foreign language. After you mark the text as foreign language text, Office can spellcheck it with the proper dictionaries. Follow these steps to mark text so that Office knows in which language it was written:

✓ Select the text that you wrote in a foreign language.

✓ Go to the Review tab.

✓ Click the Language button and choose Set Proofing Language on the drop-down list.

✓ Select a language and click OK.

Marking text as foreign language text

Points to Remember

☞ Microsoft Office provides limited support to the regional languages
☞ Download fonts and custom dictionaries for your regional languages separately
☞ Practise your regional keyboard thoroughly
☞ Use spelling & grammar checker for best results
☞ Use Thesaurus for saving your time

5th Chapter

Tables

In this chapter you will learn

- Using table tools
- Utilising other Table Resources

Before starting the Course you need to know the following terms:

❑ **Cell:** The box that is formed where a row and column intersect. Each cell holds one data item.

❑ **Header row:** The name of the labels along the top row that explain what is in the columns below.

❑ **Row labels:** The labels in the first column that describe what is in each row.

❑ **Borders:** The lines in the table that define where the rows and columns are.

❑ **Gridlines:** The gray lines that show where the columns and rows are.

Unless you've drawn borders around all the cells in a table, you can't tell where rows and columns begin and end without gridlines. To display or hide the gridlines, go to the (Table Tools) Layout tab and click the View Gridlines button.

Creating a Table

❑ **Drag on the Table menu:** On the Insert tab, click the Table button, point in the drop-down list to the number of columns and rows you want, click, and let go of the mouse button.

Row labels	Header row			
	Qtr 1	Qtr 2	Qtr 3	Qtr 4
East	4	8	5	6
West	3	4	4	9
North	3	8	9	6
South	8	7	7	9

Borders   Gridlines   Cells

❑ **Use the Insert Table dialog box:** On the Insert tab, click the Table button and choose Insert Table on the drop-down list. The Insert Table dialog box appears. Enter the number of columns and rows you want and click OK. In PowerPoint, you can also open the Insert Table dialog box by clicking the Table icon in a content placeholder frame.

❑ **Draw a table (Word and PowerPoint):** On the Insert tab, click the Table button and then choose Draw Table on the drop-down list. The pointer changes into a pencil. Use the pencil to draw table borders, rows, and columns. If you make a mistake, click the Eraser button on the (Table Tools) Design tab and drag it over the parts of the table you regret drawing (you may have to click the Draw Borders button first). When you finish drawing the table, press Esc. You can click the Pen Colour button and choose a colour on the drop-down list to draw your table in your favourite colour.

❑ **Create a quick table (Word):** On the Insert tab, click the Table button and choose Quick Tables on the drop-down list. Then choose a readymade table on the submenu. You have to replace the sample data in the quick table with your own data.

❑ **Convert text in a list into a table (Word):** Press Tab or enter a comma in each list item where you want the columns in the table to be. Select the text you'll convert to a table, click the Table button on the Insert tab, and choose Convert Text to Table. Under Separate Text At in the Convert Text to Table dialog box, choose Tabs or Commas to tell Word how the columns are separated. Then click OK.

Entering Text and Numbers

After you create the table, you can start entering text and numbers. All you have to do is click in a cell and start typing. Select your table and take advantage of these methods to make the onerous task of entering table data a little easier:

❑ **Quickly changing a table's size:** Drag the bottom or side of a table to change its overall size. In Word, you can also go to the (Table Tools) Layout tab, click the AutoFit button, and choose AutoFit Window to make the table stretch from margin to margin.

❑ **Moving a table:** In Word, switch to Print Layout view and drag the table selector (the square in the upper-left corner of the table). In PowerPoint and Publisher, move the pointer over the table's perimeter, and when you see the four-headed arrow, click and drag.

❑ **Choosing your preferred font and font size:** Entering table data is easier when you're working in a font and font size you like. Select the table, visit the Home tab, and choose a font and font size there. In Word and PowerPoint, you can select a table by going to the (Table Tools) Layout tab, clicking the Select button, and choosing Select Table on the drop-down list.

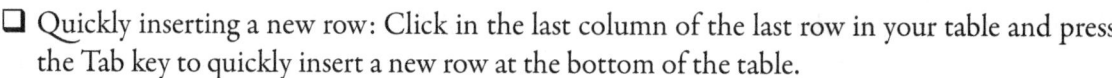

❏ **Quickly inserting a new row:** Click in the last column of the last row in your table and press the Tab key to quickly insert a new row at the bottom of the table.

Selecting different parts of a Table

❏ **Selecting cells:** To select a cell, click it. You can select several adjacent cells by dragging the pointer over them.

❏ **Selecting rows:** Move the pointer to the left of the row and click when you see the right-pointing arrow; click and drag to select several rows. You can also go to the (Table Tools) Layout tab, click inside the row you want to select, click the Select button, and choose Select Row on the drop-down list. To select more than one row at a time, select cells in the rows before choosing the Select Row command.

❏ **Selecting columns:** Move the pointer above the column and click when you see the down-pointing arrow; click and drag to select several columns. You can also start from the (Table Tools) Layout tab, click in the column you want to select, click the Select button, and choose Select Column in the drop-down list. To select several columns, select cells in the columns before choosing the Select Column command.

❏ **Selecting a table:** On the (Table Tools) Layout tab, click the Select button, and choose Select Table on the drop-down list. In PowerPoint, you can also right-click a table and choose Select Table on the shortcut menu.

Merging and Splitting Cells

Merge cells to break down the barriers between cells and join them into one cell; split cells to divide a single cell into several cells (or severalcells into several more cells).

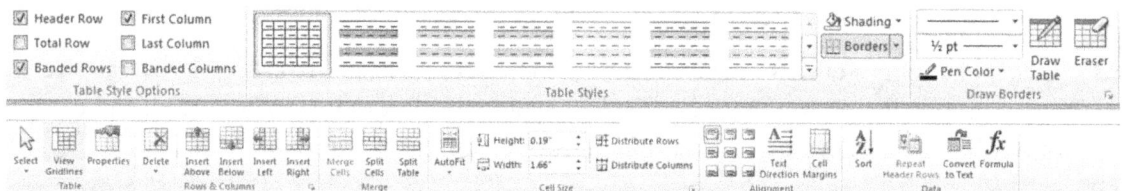

❏ Select the cells you want to merge or split, go to the (Table Tools) Layout tab, and follow these instructions to merge or split cells:

✓ **Merging cells:** Click the Merge Cells button (in Word and PowerPoint, you can also right-click and choose Merge Cells).

✓ **Splitting cells:** Click the Split Cells button (in Word and PowerPoint, you can also right-click and choose Split Cells). In the Split Cells dialog box, declare how many columns and rows you want to split the cell into and then click OK. In Publisher, you can only split cells that were previously merged.

Laying Out your Table

❑ **Column or row:** Move the pointer onto a gridline or border, and when the pointer changes into a double-headed arrow, start dragging. Tug and pull, tug and pull until the column or row is the right size. In Word and PowerPoint, you can also go to the (Table Tools) Layout tab and enter measurements in the Height and Width text boxes to change the width of a column or the height of a row. The measurements affect entire columns or rows, not individual cells.

❑ **A table:** Select your table and use one of these techniques to change its size in Word and PowerPoint:

❑ **Dragging:** Drag the top, bottom, or side of the table. You can also drag the lower-right corner to change the size vertically and horizontally.

❑ **Height and Width text boxes:** On the (Table Tools) Layout tab, enter measurements in the Height and Width text boxes. In Publisher, these text boxes are found on the (Table Tools) Design tab. In PowerPoint, click the Lock Aspect Ratio check box if you want to keep the table's proportions when you change its height or width.

❑ **Table Properties dialog box (Word only):** On the (Table Tools) Layout tab, click the Cell Size group button, and on the Table tab of the Table Properties dialog box, enter a measurement in the Preferred Width text box.

Adjusting Column and Row size

Resizing columns and rows can be problematic in Word and PowerPoint. For that reason, Word and PowerPoint offer special commands on the (Table Tools) Layout tab for adjusting the width and height of rows and columns:

❑ **Making all columns the same width:** Click the Distribute Columns button to make all columns the same width. Select columns before giving this command to make only the columns you select the same width.

❑ **Making all rows the same height:** Click the Distribute Rows button to make all rows in the table the same height. Select rows before clicking the button to make only the rows you select the same height. In Word, you can also click the AutoFit button on the (Table Tools) Layout tab, and take advantage of these commands on the drop-down list for handling columns and rows.

❑ **AutoFit Contents:** Make each column wide enough to accommodate its widest entry.

- ❑ **AutoFit Window:** Stretch the table so that it fits across the page between the left and right margin.
- ❑ **Fixed Column Width:** Fix the column widths at their current settings.

Inserting and deleting columns and rows

- ❑ **Inserting columns:** Select a column or columns and click the Insert Left or Insert Right button. If you want to insert just one column, click in a column and then click the Insert Left or Insert Right button. You can also right-click, choose Insert, and choose an Insert Columns command.
- ❑ **Inserting rows:** Select a row or rows and click the Insert Above or Insert Below button. If you want to insert just one row, click in a row and click the Insert Above or Insert Below button. You can also right-click, choose Insert, and choose an Insert Rows command on the shortcut menu. To insert a row at the end of a table, move the pointer into the last cell in the last row and press the Tab key.
- ❑ **Deleting columns:** Click in the column you want to delete, click the Delete button, and choose Delete Columns on the drop-down list. Select more than one column to delete more than one. (Pressing the Delete key deletes the data in the column, not the column itself.)
- ❑ **Deleting rows:** Click in the row you want to delete, click the Delete button, and choose Delete Rows. Select more than one row to delete more than one. (Pressing the Delete key deletes the data in the row, not the row itself.)

Moving Columns and Rows

To move a column or row:

- ❑ Select the column or row you want to move. Earlier in this chapter, "Selecting Different Parts of a Table" explains how to select columns and rows.
- ❑ Right-click in the selection and choose Cut on the shortcut menu. The column or row is moved to the Clipboard.
- ❑ Insert a new column or row where you want the column or row to be. Earlier in this chapter, "Inserting and deleting columns and rows" explains how.

Move the whole column or row:

- ❑ **Column:** Click in the topmost cell in your new column and then click the Paste button or press Ctrl+V.
- ❑ **Row:** Click in the first column of the row you inserted and then click the Paste button or press Ctrl+V.

Designing a table with a table style

Click anywhere in your table and follow these steps to choose a table style:

✓ Go to the (Table Tools) Design tab.

✓ Open the Table Styles gallery and move the pointer over table style choices to "live-preview" the table. In Publisher, this gallery is called Table Formats.

✓ Select a table style. To remove a table style, open the Table Styles gallery and choose Clear (in Word) or Clear Table (in PowerPoint).

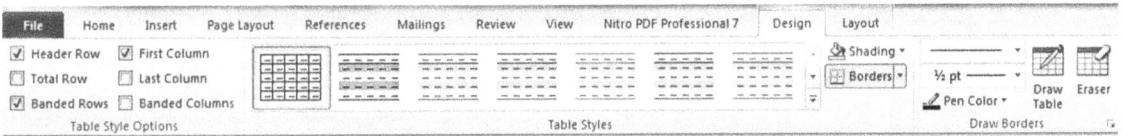

Designing borders for your table

Follow these steps to fashion a border for your table or a part of your table:

✓ Go to the (Table Tools) Design tab.

✓ Select the part of your table that needs a new border.

To select the entire table, go to the (Table Tools) Layout tab, click the Select button, and choose Select Table.

✓ Open the Line Style drop-down list (in Word) or the Pen Style drop down list (in PowerPoint) and choose a line style for the border (you may have to click the Draw Borders button first, depending on the size of your screen). Stay away from the dotted and dashed lines unless you have a good reason for choosing one. These lines can be distracting and keep others from focusing on the data presented in the table.

✓ Open the Line Weight drop-down list (in Word and Publisher) or the Pen Weight drop-down list (in PowerPoint) and choose a thickness for the border (you may have to click the Draw Borders button first).

✓ If you want your borders to be of another colour apart from black, click the Pen Colour button (Word and PowerPoint) or the Line Colour button (Publisher) and choose a colour on the drop-down list (you may have to click the Draw Borders button first).

✓ Open the drop-down list on the Borders button and choose where to place borders on the part of the table you selected in Step 2.

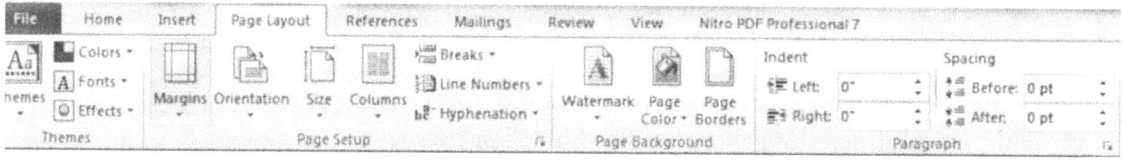

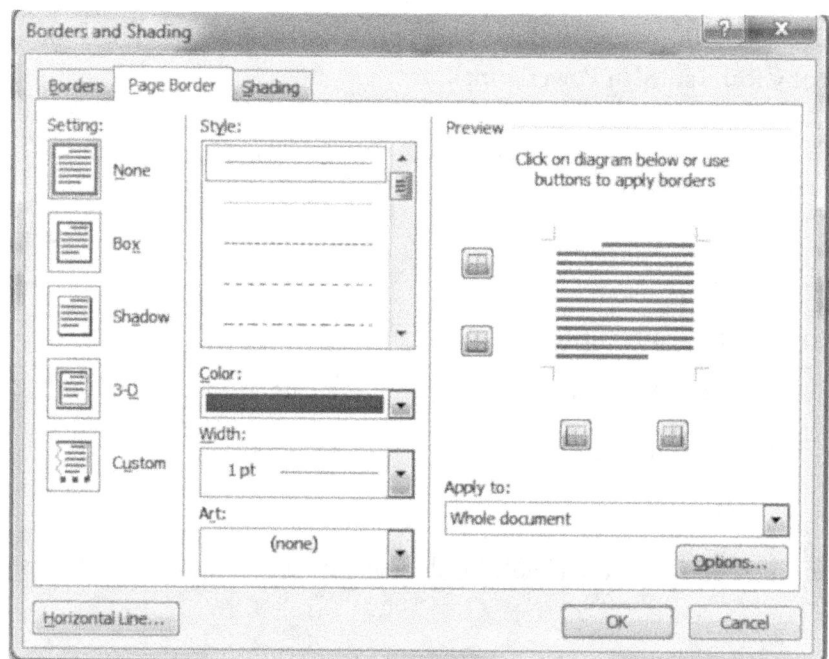

Using Math Formulas in Word Tables

You don't have to add the figures in columns and rows yourself; Word gladly does that for you. Word can perform other mathematical calculationsas well. Follow these steps to perform mathematical calculations and tell Word how to format sums and products:

✓ Put the cursor in the cell that will hold the sum or product of the cells above, below, to the right, or to the left.

✓ On the (Table Tools) Layout tab, click the Formula button.

Drawing diagonal lines on tables

Draw diagonal lines across table cells to cancel out those cells or otherwise make cells look different.

- ❑ **Draw Table button:** Click the Draw Table button (you may have to click the Draw Borders button first). The pointer changes into a pencil. Drag to draw the diagonal lines. Press Esc or click the Draw Table button a second time when you're finished drawing. Click the Pen Colour button and choose a colour before drawing on your table if you want the diagonal lines to be of certain colour.

- ❑ **Borders button:** Select the cells that need diagonal lines, open the dropdown list on the Borders button, and choose Diagonal down Border or Diagonal Up Border.

Drawing on a Table

- ✓ On the Insert tab, click the Shapes button and select the Oval shape on the drop-down list.

- ✓ On a corner of your page or slide, away from the table, drag to draw the oval.

- ✓ On the (Drawing Tools) Format tab, open the drop-down list on the Shape Fill button and choose No Fill.

- ✓ Open the drop-down list on the Shape Outline button and choose a very dark colour.

- ✓ Open the drop-down list on the Shape Outline button, choose Weight, and choose a thick line.

- ✓ Drag the oval over the data on your table that you want to highlight. If the oval is obscured by the table, go to the (Drawing Tools) Format tab, and click the Bring Forward button (click the Arrange button, if necessary, to see this button). While you're at it, consider rotating the oval a little way to make it appear as though it was drawn by hand on the table.

Points to Remember

- ☞ Use table resources carefully
- ☞ Keep an eye on margins while drawing tables

Charts

In this chapter you will learn

- Using Charts
- Creating & designing charts
- Using other Graphical effects in your file

Anatomy of Charts

Before you start doing activities on charts, you need to know the following:

❑ **Plot area:** The center of the chart, apart from the legend and data labels, where the data itself is presented.

❑ **Values:** The numerical values with which the chart is plotted. The values you enter determine the size of the data markers — the bars, columns, pie slices, and so on — that portray values.

❑ **Gridlines:** Lines on the chart that indicate value measurements. Gridlines are optional in charts.

❑ **Worksheet:** Where you enter (or retrieve) the data used to plot the chart. The worksheet resembles a table. A worksheet is called a data table when it appears along with a chart.

❑ **Data series:** A group of related data points presented by category on a chart.

❑ **Categories:** The actual items that you want to compare or display in your chart.

❑ **Legend:** A text box located to the side, top, or bottom of a chart that identifies the chart's data labels.

❑ **Horizontal and vertical axes:** For plotting purposes, one side of the plot area.

❑ **Data point:** A value plotted on a chart that is represented by a column, line, bar, pie slice, dot, or other shape.

❏ **Data marker:** Shapes on a chart that represents data points.

❏ **Data label:** A label that shows the actual values used to construct the data markers.

The Basics: Creating a Chart

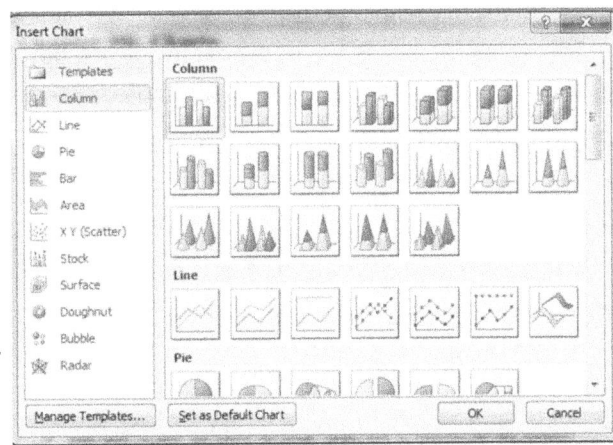

✓ Go to the Insert tab.

✓ If you're working in Excel, select the data you'll use to generate the chart.

✓ Select the kind of chart you want.

✓ To modify your chart, start by selecting it. Click a chart to select it. Selecting a chart makes the Chart Tools tabs appear in the upper-right corner of the window. Use these tabs — Design, Layout, and Format — to make your chart just-so. In Word, you must be in Print Layout view to see a chart.

✓ Select the (Chart Tools) Design tab when you want to change the chart's layout, alter the data with which the chart was generated, or select a different chart type.

✓ Select the (Chart Tools) Layout tab when you want to change the chart's title, labels, or gridlines. You can add or remove parts of a chart starting on the Layout tab.

✓ Select the (Chart Tools) Format tab when you want to change the appearance of your chart.

Changing chart layout

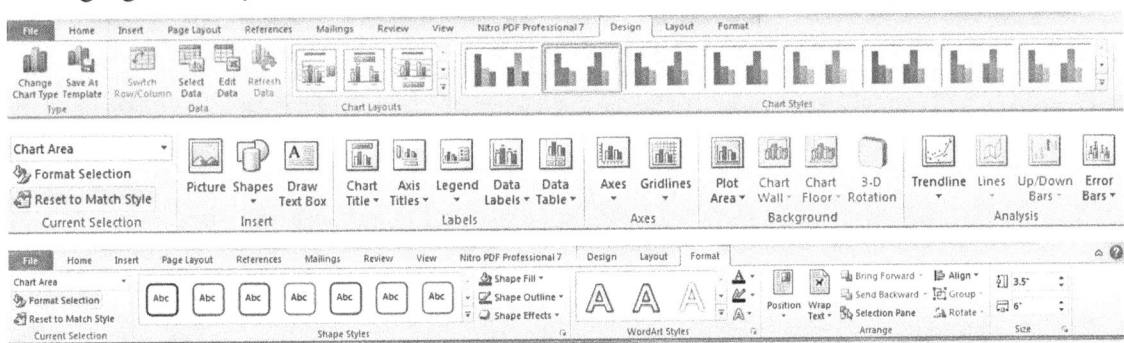

❏ **Design tab:** For quickly changing a chart's appearance, go to the Design tab. The ready-made gallery choices give you the opportunity to change a chart's layout and appearance in a matter of seconds. You can also choose a new chart type from the Design tab.

❑ **Layout tab:** For rearranging, hiding, and displaying various parts of a chart, including the legend, labels, title, gridlines, and scale, go to the Layout tab to tweak your chart and make different parts of it stand out or recede into the background.

❑ **Format tab:** For changing the colour, outline, font, and font size of various parts of a chart, including the labels, bars, and pie slices, you have to really know what you're doing and have a lot of time on your hands to change colours and fonts throughout a chart.

Changing Chart Type

✓ Click your chart to select it.

✓ On the (Chart Tools) Design tab, click the Change Chart Type button, or right-click your chart and choose Change Chart Type on the shortcut menu.

✓ Select a new chart type and click OK.

Changing Size and Shape of a Chart

To make a chart taller or wider, follow these instructions:

✓ Click the perimeter of the chart to select it and then drag a handle on the side to make it wider, or a handle on the top or bottom to make it taller.

✓ Go to the (Chart Tools) Format tab and enter measurements in the Shape Height and Shape Width boxes. You can find these boxes in the Size group (you may have to click the Size button to see them, depending on the size of your screen).

Relying on A Chart Style to change appearances

The easiest way to change the look of a chart is to choose an option in the Chart Styles gallery in the (Chart Tools) Design tab.

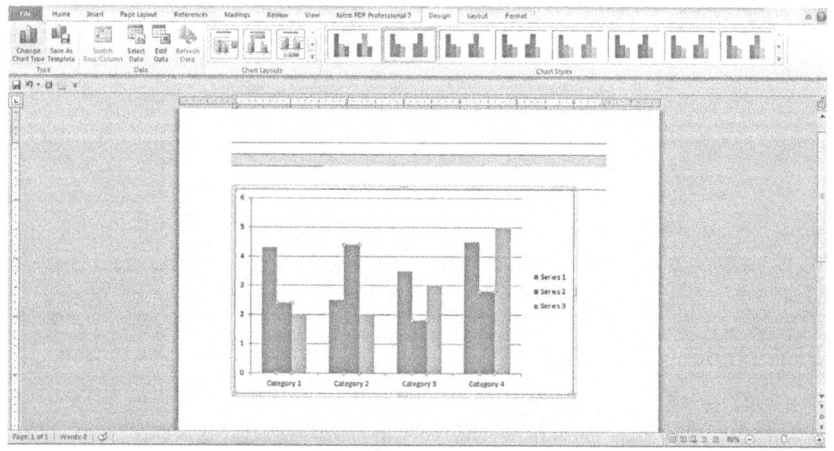

Changing a Chart elements' colour, font, or other particular

✓ Select the (Chart Tools) Format tab. The tools on the (Chart Tools) Format tab are very similar to the tools found on the (Drawing Tools) Format tab. You can find all the tools you need here to change the colour, outline, and size of a chart element.

✓ Select the chart element that needs a facelift. To select a chart element, either click it or choose its name on the Chart Elements drop-down.

✓ Format the chart element you selected.

Use one of these methods to format the chart element:

✓ Open a Format dialog box. The dialog box offers commands for formatting the element you selected.

✓ Do the work on your own. For example, to change fonts in the chart element you selected, right-click and choose a font on the shortcut menu. Or go to the Home tab to change font sizes. Or open the drop-down list on the Shape Fill button on the (Chart Tools) Format tab and select a new colour.

Saving a Chart as a Template

Follow these steps to make a template out of a chart:

✓ Save your file to make sure that the chart settings are saved on your computer.

✓ Select your chart.

✓ Go to the (Chart Tools) Design tab.

✓ Click the Save as Template button. You can find this button in the Type group. You will see the Save Chart Template dialog box.

✓ Enter a descriptive name for the template and click the Save button. Include the type of chart you're dealing with in the name. This will help you understand which template you're selecting when the time comes to choose a chart template.

Inserting a picture

✓ Select your chart.

✓ On the (Chart Tools) Format tab, open the Chart Elements drop-down list and choose Plot Area.

✓ Click the Shape Fill button and choose Picture on the drop-down list. You will see the Insert Picture dialog box.

✓ Locate the picture you need and select it. Try to select a light-coloured picture that will serve as a background.

✓ Click the Insert button. The picture lands in your chart.

Annotating a chart

✓ Select your chart and go to the (Chart Tools) Layout tab.

✓ Click the Shapes button, scroll to the Callouts section of the dropdown list, and choose a callout.

✓ Depending on the size of your screen, you may have to click the Insert button to get to the Shapes button.

✓ Drag on your slide to draw the callout shape.

✓ Type the annotation inside the callout shape.

✓ Resize the callout shape as necessary to make it fit with the chart

✓ Drag the yellow diamond on the callout shape to attach the callout to the chart.

Points to Remember

☞ Use charts judiciously & never put invalid arguments for the charts
☞ Practise Microsoft excel 2010 before making custom charts

SmartArt

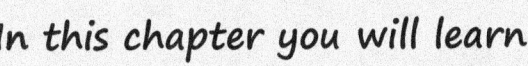

In this chapter you will learn

- Using Diagrams & shapes in file or document
- Using hybrid layouts with diagrams & Text together

Creating a diagram

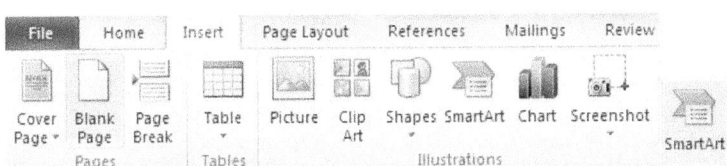

After you select a generic diagram in the Choose a SmartArt Graphic dialog box and click OK, the next step is to make the diagram your own by completing these tasks:

❑ **Change the diagram's size and position:** Change the size and position of a diagram to make it fit squarely on your page or slide. See "Changing the Size and Position of a Diagram," later in this chapter.

❑ **Add shapes to (or remove shapes from) the diagram:** Adding a shape involves declaring where to add the shape, promoting or demoting the shape with respect to other shapes, and declaring how the new shape connects to another shape. See "Laying Out the Diagram Shapes" later in this chapter.

❑ **Enter text:** Enter text on each shape, or component, of the diagram. See "Handling the Text on Diagram Shapes" later in this chapter. If you so desire, you can also customize your diagram by taking on some oral of these tasks:

- ❑ **Changing its overall appearance:** Choose a different colour scheme or 3-D variation for your diagram. See "Choosing a Look for Your Diagram" later in this chapter.

- ❑ **Changing shapes:** Select a new shape for part of your diagram, change the size of a shape, or assign different colours to shapes to make shapes stand out. See "Changing the Appearance of Diagram Shapes" later in this chapter.

Creating a diagram

Follow these steps to create a diagram:

- ✓ On the Insert tab, click the SmartArt button. You will see the Choose a SmartArt Graphic dialog box; you can also open the dialog box by clicking the SmartArt Icon in a content placeholder frame.

- ✓ Select a diagram in the Choose a SmartArt Graphic dialog box. Diagrams are divided into eight categories.

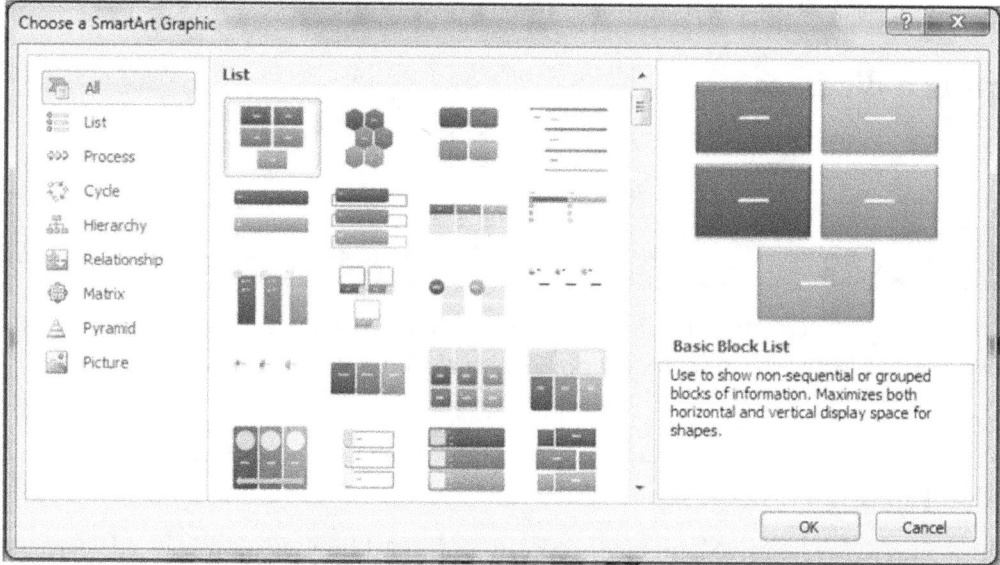

- ✓ Click your diagram to select it.

- ✓ Go to the (SmartArt Tools) Design tab.

- ✓ Open the Layouts gallery (you may have to click the Change Layout button first).You will see a gallery with diagrams of the same type as the diagram you're working with. Select a new diagram or choose More Layouts to open the Choose a SmartArt Graphic dialog box and select a diagram there.

Changing Size and Position of a diagram

To make a diagram fit squarely on a page or slide, you have to change its size and position.

❑ **Resizing a diagram:** Select the diagram, move the pointer over a selection handle on the corner or side, and start dragging after the pointer changes into a two-headed arrow. You can also go to the (SmartArt Tools) Format tab and enter new measurements in the Width and Height boxes. (You may have to click the Size button to see these text boxes, depending on the size of your screen.)

❑ **Repositioning a diagram:** Select the diagram, move the pointer over its perimeter, and when you see the four-headed arrow, click and start dragging.

Adding shapes to diagrams apart from hierarchy diagrams

Follow these steps to add a shape to a list, process, cycle, relationship, matrix, or pyramid diagram:

✓ In your diagram, select the shape that your new shape will appear before or after.

✓ Choose the Add Shape After or Add Shape Before command. To get to these commands, use one of these methods:

   ✓ On the (SmartArt Tools) Design tab, open the drop-down list on the Add Shape button and choose Add Shape After or Add Shape Before.

   ✓ Right-click the shape you selected, choose Add Shape on the shortcut menu, and then choose Add Shape After or Add Shape Before on the submenu.

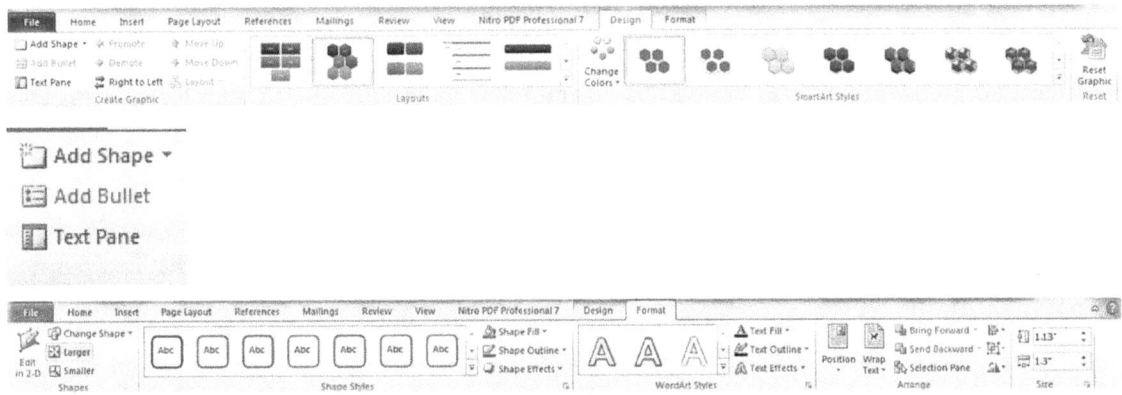

Adding an Organization Chart shape

Besides adding a shape after, before, above, or below a shape, you can add an assistant shape to an Organization Chart diagram. An assistant shape is an intermediary shape between two levels. Follow these steps to add a shape to an Organization Chart diagram:

- ✓ Select the shape to which you will add a new shape.

- ✓ Choose an Add Shape command.

You can choose Add Shape commands in two ways:

- ✓ On the (SmartArt Tools) Design tab, open the drop-down list on the Add Shape button and choose an Add Shape command.

- ✓ Right-click the shape you selected, choose Add Shape on the shortcut menu, and then choose an Add Shape command on the submenu.

Entering text on a diagram shape

Use one of these techniques to enter text on a diagram shape:

- ✓ Click on the shape and start typing: The words you type appear.

- ✓ Enter text in the Text pane: Enter the text by typing it in the Text pane

- ✓ On the (SmartArt Tools) Design tab, click the Text Pane button.

- ✓ Click the Text Pane button on the diagram. This button is not labeled, but you can find it to the left of the diagram.

Entering bulleted lists on diagram shapes

Some diagram shapes have built-in bulleted lists, but no matter. Whether a shape is prepared to be bulleted or not, you can enter bullets in a diagram shape. Here are instructions for entering and removing bullets:

- ❑ **Entering a bulleted list:** Select the shape that needs bullets, and on the (SmartArt Tools) Design tab, click the Add Bullet button. Either enter the bulleted items directly into the shape (pressing Enter as you type each entry) or click the Text Pane button to open the Text pane.

- ❑ **Removing bulleted items:** Click before the first bulleted entry and keep pressing the Delete key until you have removed all the bulleted items.

Changing a Diagram's direction

- ✓ Select the diagram.

- ✓ On the (SmartArt Tools) Design tab, click the Right to Left button. If you don't like what you see, click the button again or click the Undo button.

Changing the size of a diagram shape

Select your shape and use one of these methods to enlarge or shrink it:

✓ On the (SmartArt Tools) Format tab, click the Larger or Smaller buttonas many times as necessary to make the shape the right size.

✓ Move the pointer over a corner selection handle, and when the pointer changes to a two-headed arrow, click and start dragging.

Points to Remember

☞ Choose the size of your diagrams judiciously so that it can blend with text perfectly

☞ Make your chart more descriptive by adding hybrid effects

☞ Select the flow-charts wisely

Drawing Lines & other Shapes

In this chapter you will learn

- Ways to manipulate lines, shapes, text boxes, WordArt images, clip-art images, and graphics

The Basics: Drawing Lines, Arrows, and Shapes

Follow these basic steps to draw a line, arrow, or shape:

✓ Go to the Insert tab.

✓ Click the Shapes button to open the Insert Shapes gallery.

✓ Select a line, arrow, or shape in the Shapes gallery.

✓ Drag on your page, slide, or worksheet. As you drag, the line, arrow, or shape appears.

✓ To alter your line, arrow, or shape—that is, to change its size, colour, or outline—go to the (Drawing Tools) Format tab. This tab offers many commands for manipulating lines and shapes.

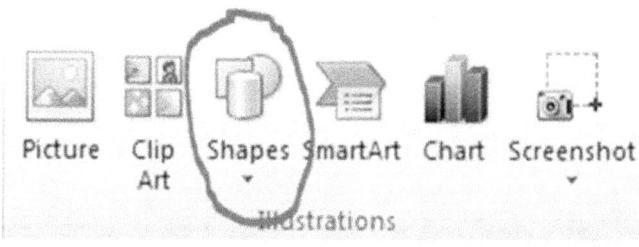

Handling Lines, Arrows, and Connectors

Changing the length and position of a line or arrow

To change anything about a line or arrow, start by clicking to select it. You can tell when a line has been selected because round selection handles appear at either end. Follow these instructions to move a line or adjust its length or angle:

❑ **Changing the angle of a line:** Drag a selection handle up, down, or sideways. A dotted line shows where your line will be when you release the mouse button.

❑ **Changing the length:** Drag a selection handle away from or toward the opposite selection handle.

❑ **Changing the position:** Move the pointer over the line itself and click when you see the four-headed arrow. Then drag the line to a new location.

Changing the appearance of a line, arrow, or connector

What a line looks like is a matter of its colour, its weight (how wide it is), its dash status (it can be filled out or dashed), and its cap (its ends can berounded, square, or flat). To change the appearance of a line, start by selecting it, going to the (Drawing Tools) Format tab, and opening the drop-down list on the Shape Outline button (this button is in the Shape Styles group).

❑ **Colour:** Select a colour on the drop-down list.

❑ **Width:** Choose Weight on the drop-down and then choose a line width on the submenu. You can also choose More Lines on the submenu to open the Format Shape dialog box and change the width there. Enter a setting in points to make the line heavier or thinner.

❑ **Dotted or dashed lines:** Choose Dashes on the drop-down list and then choose an option on the submenu. Again, you can choose More Lines to open the Format Shape dialog box and choose from many dash types and compound lines.

❑ **Line caps:** Click the Shape Styles group button to open the Format Shape dialog box. In the Line Style category, select a cap type (Square, Round, or Flat).

Making the connection

Before you draw the connections, draw the shapes and arrange them on the slide where you want them to be in your diagram. Then follow these steps to connect two shapes with a connector:

✓ Select the two shapes that you want to connect. To select the shapes, hold down the Ctrl key and click each one.

- ✓ On the (Drawing Tools) Format tab, open the Shapes gallery.

- ✓ Under Lines, select the connector that will best fit between the two shapes you want to link together.

- ✓ Move the pointer over a side selection handle on one of the shapes you want to connect. The selection handles turn red.

- ✓ Click and drag the pointer over a selection handle on the other shape, and when you see red selection handles on that shape, release the mouse button. Red, round selection handles appear on the shapes where they're connected. These red handles tell you that the two shapes are connected and will remain connected when you move them.

Handling Rectangles, Ovals, Stars, and Other Shapes

Drawing a shape

Follow these steps to draw a shape:

- ✓ On the Insert tab, click the Shapes button to open the Shapes gallery. You can also insert shapes from the Shapes gallery on the (Drawing Tools) Format tab.

- ✓ Select a shape in the gallery. If you've drawn the shape recently, you may be able to find it at the top of the gallery under Recently Used Shapes.

- ✓ Click and drag slantwise to draw the shape. Hold down the Shift key as you drag if you want the shape to retain its proportions. For example, to draw a circle, select the Oval shape and Hold down the Shift key as you draw.

Changing a shape's size and shape

Selection handles appear on the corners and sides of a shape after you select it. With the selection handles showing, you can change a shape's size and shape:

- ✓ Hold down the Shift key and drag a corner handle to change a shape's size and retain its symmetry.

- ✓ Drag a side, top, or bottom handle to stretch or scrunch a shape.

Choosing a different shape

To exchange one shape for another, select the shape and follow these steps:

- ✓ On the (Drawing Tools) Format tab, click the Edit Shape button.

- ✓ You can find this button in the Insert Shapes group.

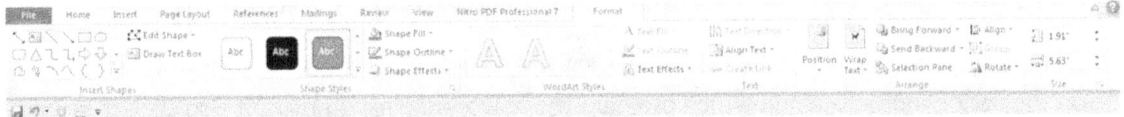

✓ Choose Change Shape on the drop-down list.

✓ Select a new shape in the Shapes gallery.

Changing a shape's symmetry

A yellow diamond, sometimes more than one, appears on some shapes. By dragging a diamond, you can change a shape's symmetry.

Follow these instructions to handle text box shapes:

❑ **Entering the text:** Click in the shape and start typing. In Word, you can right-click and choose Add Text if you have trouble typing in the shape.

❑ **Editing the text:** Click in the text and start editing. That's all there is to it. If you have trouble getting inside the shape to edit the text, select the shape, right-click it, and choose Edit Text on the shortcut menu.

❑ **Changing the font, colour, and size of text:** Right-click in the text and choose Font. Then, in the Font dialog box, choose a font, font colour, and a font size for the text.

WordArt for Bending, Spindling, and Mutilating Text

❑ **Allowing the shape to enlarge for text:** You can allow the shape to enlarge and receive more text. Click the Shape Styles group button, and in the Text Box category of the Format Shape dialog box, select the Resize Shape to Fit Text option button.

Creating a WordArt image

Follow these steps to create a WordArt image:

✓ On the Insert tab, click the WordArt button. A drop-down list with WordArt styles appears.

✓ Select a WordArt style.

✓ Enter the text for the image in the WordArt text box.

Editing a WordArt image

On the (Drawing Tools) Format tab, click the Edit Shape button, choose Change Shape, and then select a shape in the Shapes gallery. After the conversion, you usually have to enlarge the shape to

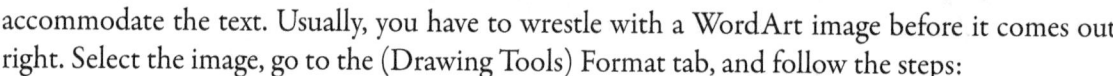

accommodate the text. Usually, you have to wrestle with a WordArt image before it comes out right. Select the image, go to the (Drawing Tools) Format tab, and follow the steps:

❑ **Editing the words:** Click in the WordArt text box and edit the text there.

❑ **Choosing a new WordArt style:** Open the WordArt Styles gallery and select a style. Depending on the size of your screen and which program you're working in, you may have to click the Quick Styles button first

❑ **Changing the letters' colour:** Click the Text Fill button and choose a colour on the drop-down list.

❑ **Changing the letters' outline:** Click the Text Outline button and make choices to change the letters' outline.

Points to Remember

☞ Practise the skills thoroughly
☞ Don't Use too much formatting.

Microsoft
Power Point
2010

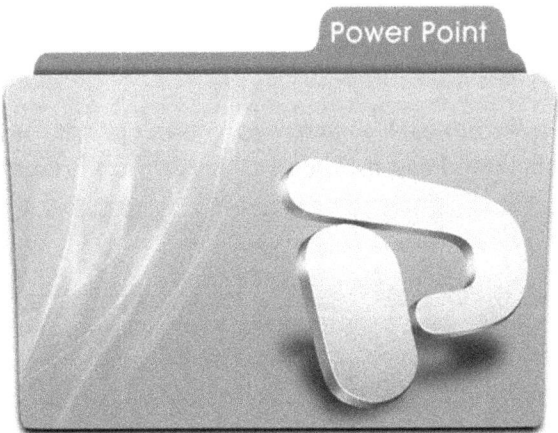

Chapter

Welcome to MS PowerPoint 2010

In this chapter you will learn

- Getting started with the PowerPoint screen
- Creating a Slide show
- Changing your view of a document
- Selecting text so that you can copy, move, or delete it
- Getting from place to place in long documents
- Pasting one slide document into another

It is practically impossible to sit through a conference, seminar, or trade show without seeing at least one PowerPoint presentation. PowerPoint has found its way into nearly every office and boardroom.

Note....✍

Presentation: All the slides, from start to finish, that you show your audience. Sometimes presentations are called "slide shows." Presentations are saved in presentation files (.pptx files).

Slides: The images you create with PowerPoint. During a presentation, slides appear on-screen one after the other. Don't be put off by the word slide and dreary memories of sitting through your uncle's slide show vacation memories. You don't need a slide projector to show these slides. You can now plug a laptop or other computer into special monitors that display PowerPoint slides.

Creating PowerPoint Presentation

Creating a PowerPoint presentation entails completing these basic tasks:

❏ **Creating the slides:** Once you open the PPT Window, your next task is to create the slides. PowerPoint offers many preformatted slide layouts, each designed for presenting information a certain way.

❏ **Notes:** As you create slides, you can jot down notes in the Notes pane. You can use these notes later to formulate your presentation and decide what you're going to say to your audience while each slide is on-screen.

❏ **Designing your presentation:** After you create a presentation, the next step is to think about its appearance. You can change slides' colours and backgrounds, as well as choose a theme for your presentation, an all-encompassing design that applies to all (or most of) the slides.

❏ **Inserting tables, charts, diagrams, and shapes:** A PowerPoint presentation should be more than a loose collection of bulleted lists. Starting on the Insert tab, you can place tables, charts, and diagrams on slides, as well as adorn your slides with text boxes, WordArt images, and shapes.

❏ **"Animating" your slides:** PowerPoint slides can play video and sound, as well as be "animated". You can make the items on a slide move on the screen. As a slide arrives, you can make it spin or flash.

❏ **Delivering your presentation:** During a presentation, you can draw on the slides. You can also blank the screen and show slides out of order. In case you can't be there in person, PowerPoint gives you the opportunity to create self-running presentations and presentations that others can run on their own. You can also distribute presentations on CDs and videos.

Creating a New Presentation

No matter what kind of presentation you want to create, start creating it by going to the File tab and choosing New. You will see the Available Templates and Themes window. This window offers templates for creating many types of presentations. Click a template to preview it on the right side of the window. Double-click a template (or select it and click the Create button) to create a presentation. Apply following methods to create a presentation:

❑ **Blank presentation:** Double-click the Blank Presentation icon. A new presentation appears. Try visiting the Design tab and choosing a theme or background style to get a taste of all the things you can do to decorate a presentation. (By pressing Ctrl+N, you can create a new, blank Presentation without opening the Available Templates and Themes window.)

❑ **Recently used template:** Click the Recent Templates icon to use a template listed there.

❑ **Template on your computer:** Click the Sample Templates icon. Templates that you loaded on your computer when you installed PowerPoint appear.

❑ **Template you created (or downloaded earlier from Microsoft):** Click the My Templates icon. The New Presentation dialog box appears. Select a template and click OK.

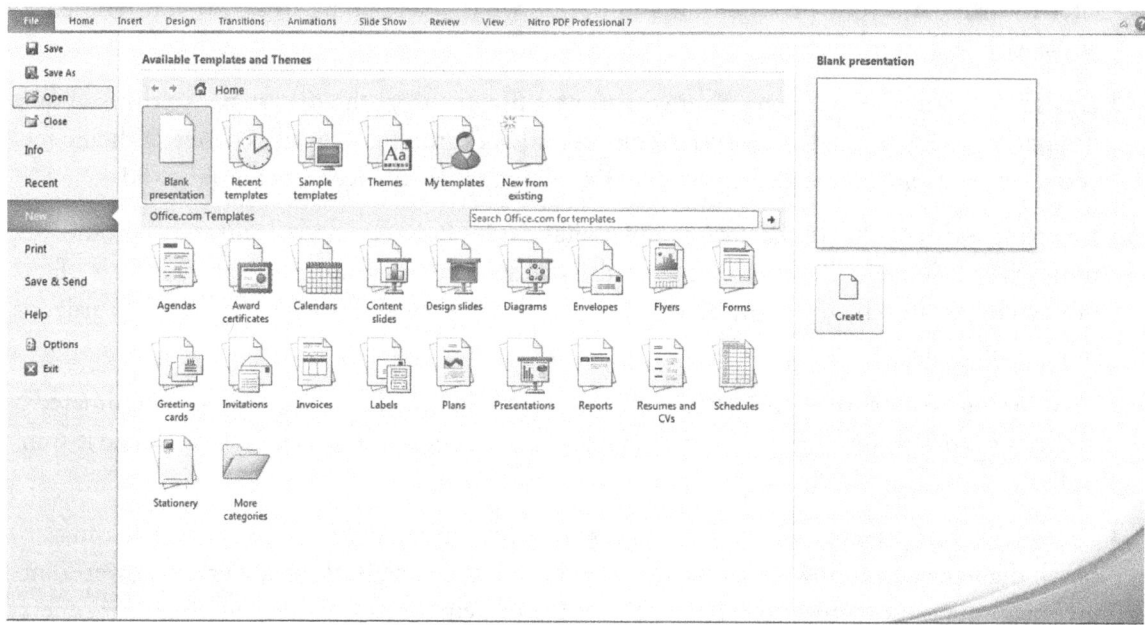

- **Template available online at Office.com:** Enter a search term in the Search box, make sure that your computer is connected to the Internet, and click the Start Searching button. Templates appear in the window. Double-click a template to download and use it to create a presentation.

- **Recycle another presentation:** If you can use another presentation as the starting point for creating a new presentation, nab slides from the other presentation. Click the New from Existing icon. In the New from ExistingPresentation dialog box, select the presentation and click the Open button.

Creating New Slides for Your Presentation

Inserting a new slide

Follow these steps to insert a new slide in your presentation:

- ✓ Select the slide that you want to insert. In Normal view, select the slide on the Slides pane. In Slide Sorter view, select the slide in the main window.

- ✓ On the Home tab, click the bottom half of the New Slide button. You see a drop-down list of slide layouts. (If you click the top half of the New Slide button, you insert a slide with the same layout as the one you selected in Step 1.)

- ✓ Select the slide layout that best approximates the slide you want to create.

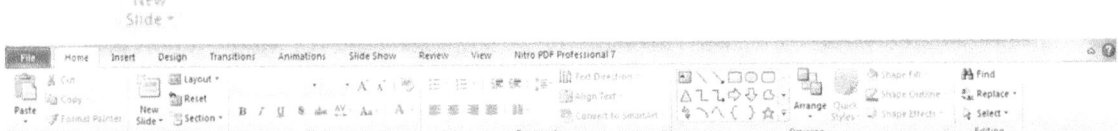

- **Creating a duplicate slide:** Select the slide or slides you want to duplicate, and on the Home tab, open the drop-down list on the New Slide button and choose Duplicate Selected Slides. You can also open the drop-down list on the Copy button and choose Duplicate.

- **Copying and pasting slides:** Click the slide you want to copy (or Ctrl+click to select more than one slide) and then click the Copy button on the Home tab (or press Ctrl+C). Next, click to select the slide that you want the copied slide (or slides) to appear after and click the Paste button (or press Ctrl+V).

- **Recycling slides from other presentations:** Select the slide that you want the recycled slides to follow in your presentation, and on the Home tab, open the drop-down list on the New Slide button and choose Reuse Slides. The Reuse Slides task pane opens. Open the drop-down list on the Browse button, choose Browse File, and select a presentation in the Browse dialog box. The Reuse Slides task pane shows thumbnail versions of slides in the presentation you selected. One at a time, click slides to add them to your presentation. You can right-click a slide and choose Insert All Slides to grab all the slides in the presentation.

Selecting a different layout for a slide

If you mistakenly choose the wrong layout for a slide, you can start all over. You can graft a new layout onto your slide with one of these techniques:

✓ On the Home tab, click the Layout button and choose a layout on the drop-down list.

✓ Right-click the slide (being careful not to right-click a frame or object), choose Layout, and choose a layout on the submenu.

You can use Reset command also.

Changing views

PowerPoint offers two places to change views:

❏ **View buttons on the status bar:** Click the View button — Normal, Slide Sorter, Slide Show, or Reading View — on the status bar to change views.

❏ **View tab:** On the View tab, click a button on the Presentation Views or Master Views group.

❏ **Normal/Slides view for examining slides:** Switch to Normal view, move the pointer to the Slides pane, and select the Slides tab when you want to examine a slide. In this view, thumbnail slides appear in the Slides pane, and you can see your slide in all its glory in the middle of the screen.

❏ **Slide Sorter view for moving and deleting slides:** In Slide Sorter view, you will see thumbnails of all the slides in the presentation (use the Zoom Slider to change the size of thumbnails). From here, moving slides around is easy, and seeing many slides simultaneously gives you a sense of whether the different slides are consistent with one another and how the whole presentation is shaping up. The slides are numbered so that you can see where they appear in a presentation.

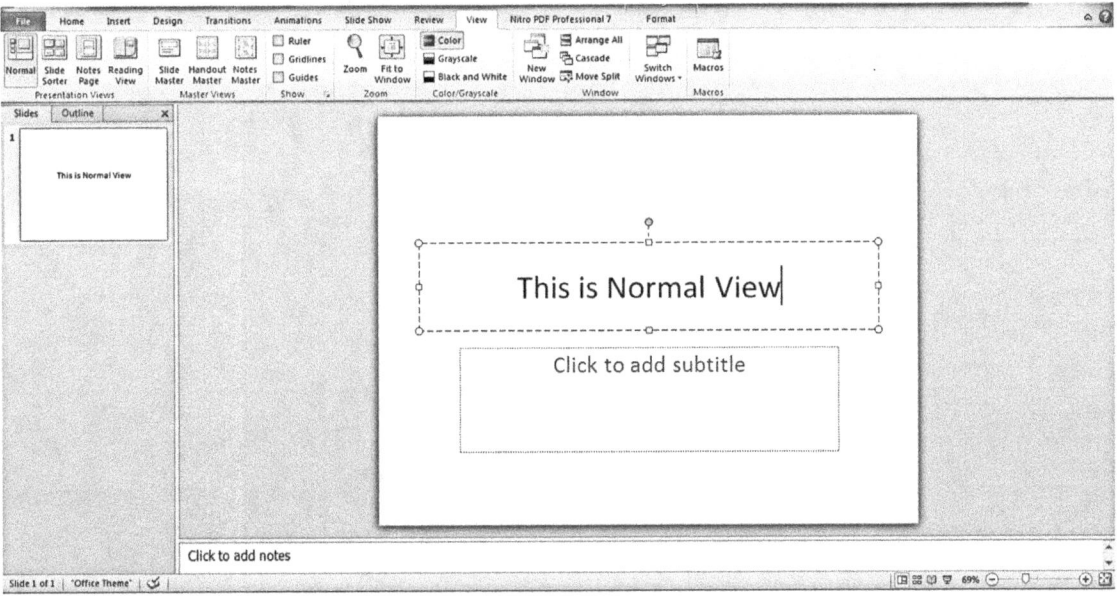

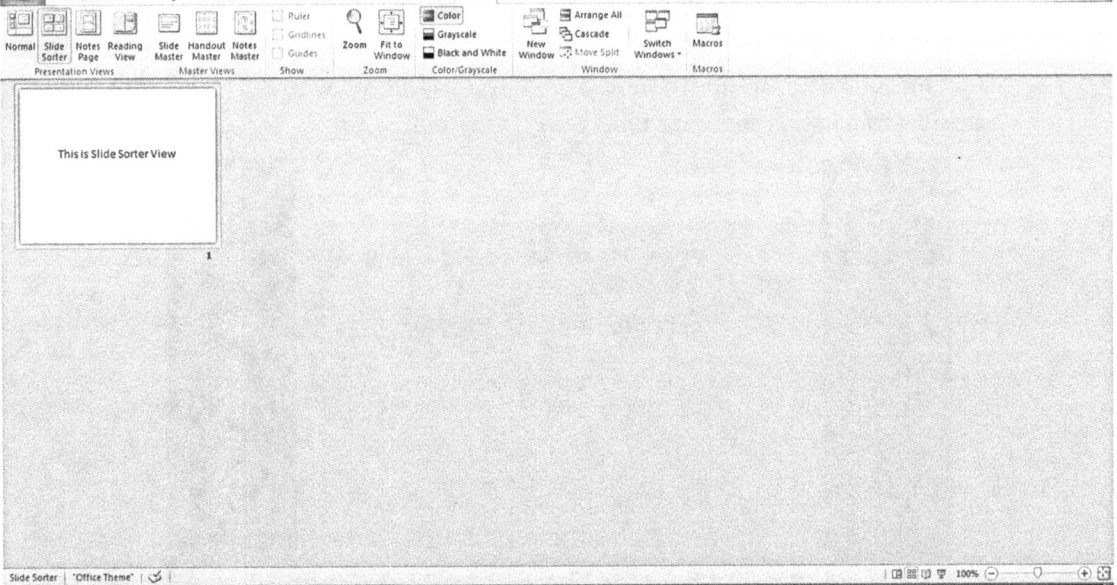

❑ **Notes Page view for reading your speaker notes:** In Notes Page view, you see notes you've written to aid you in your presentation, if you've written any. You can write notes in this view as well as in the Notes pane in Normal view.

Notes
Page

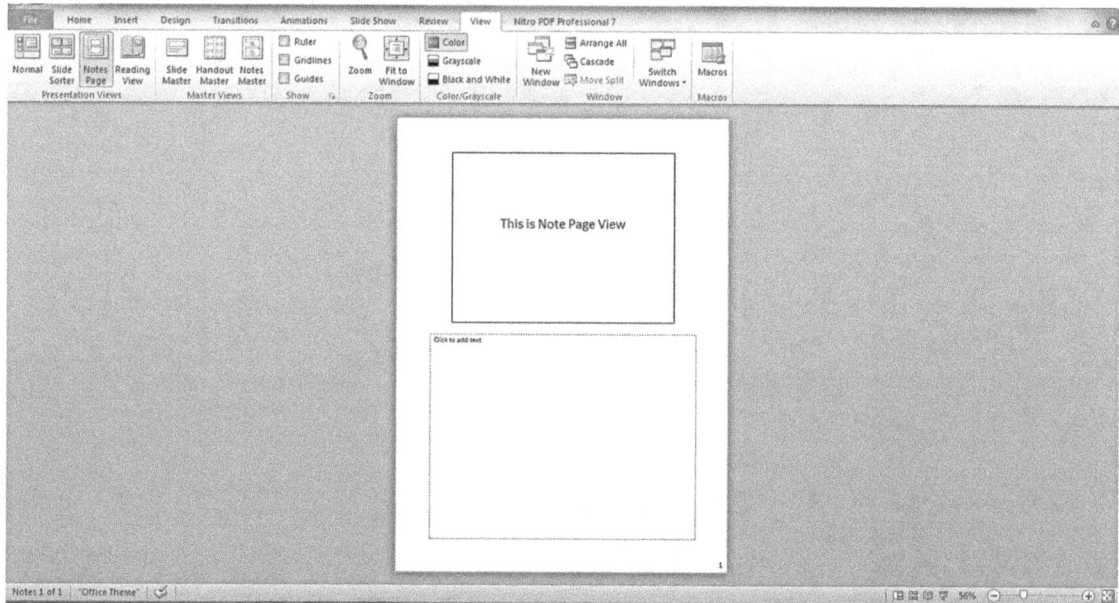

- **Reading View for focusing on slides' appearance:** In Reading View, you also see a single slide, but it appears on-screen with the View buttons and with buttons for moving quickly from slide to slide. Switch to Reading View to proofread slides and put the final touches on presentation.

- **Slide Show view for giving a presentation:** In Slide Show view, you see a single slide. Not only that, but the slide fills the entire screen. This is what your presentation looks like when you show it to an audience.

This is Slide Show View

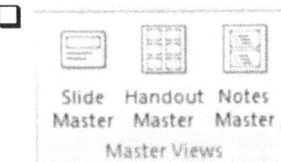

Slide Master | Handout Master | Notes Master
Master Views

The Master views for a consistent presentation: The master views — Slide Master, Handout Master, and Notes Master — are for handling master styles, the formatting commands that pertain to all the slides in a presentation, handouts, and notes. To switch to these views, go to the View tab and click the appropriate button.

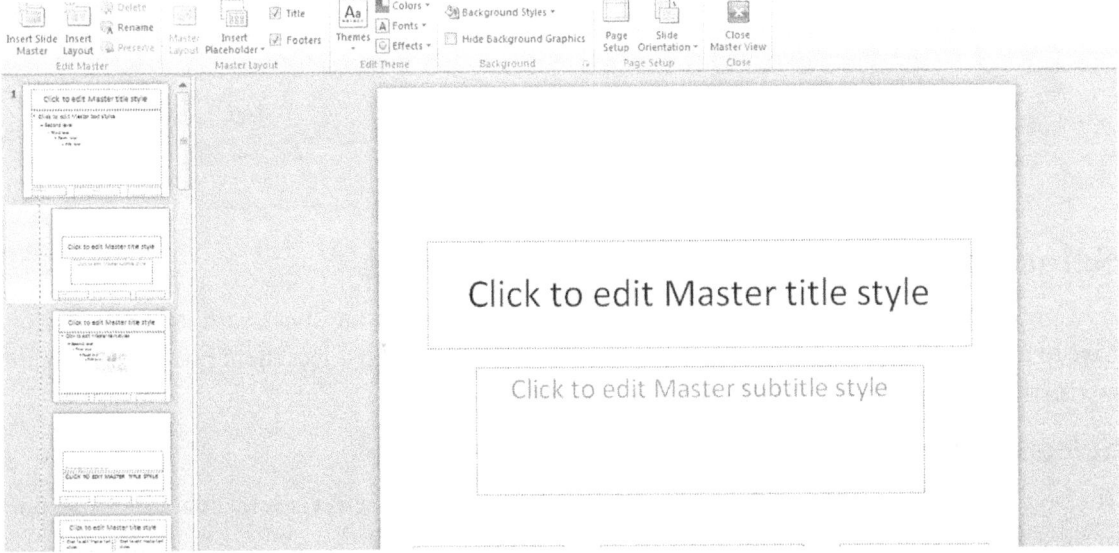

Click to edit Master title style

Click to edit Master subtitle style

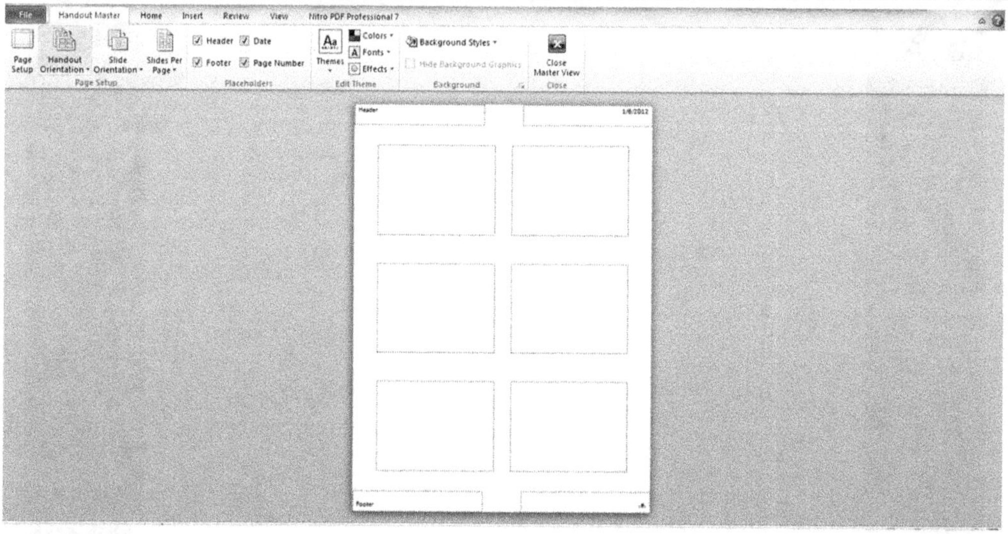

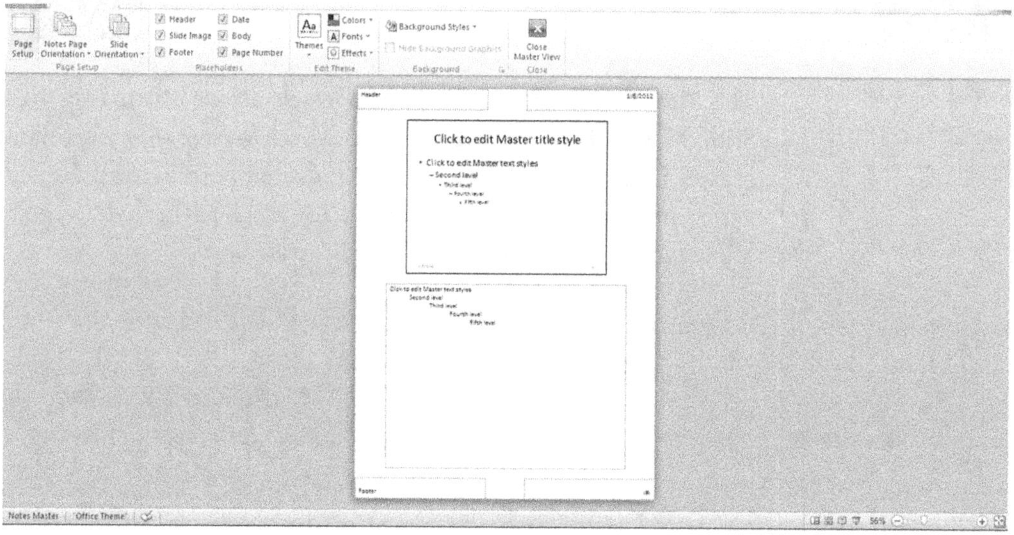

Selecting, Moving, and Deleting Slides

As a presentation takes shape, you have to move slides forward and backward. Sometimes you have to delete a slide. And you can't move or delete slides until you select them first. Herewith are instructions for selecting, moving, and deleting slides.

Selecting slides

The best place to select slides is Slide Sorter view (if you want to select several at a time). Use one of these methods to select slides:

- ❑ **Select one slide:** Click the slide.
- ❑ **Select several different slides:** Hold down the Ctrl key and click each slide in the Slides pane or in Slide Sorter view.
- ❑ **Select several slides in succession:** Hold down the Shift key and click the first slide and then the last one.

Moving slides

To move or rearrange slides, you're advised to go to Slide Sorter view. Select the slide or slides that you want to move and use one of these methods to move slides:

- ❑ **Dragging and dropping:** Click the slides you selected and drag them to a new location. You will see the drag pointer, and in Slide Sorter view, a vertical line shows you where the slide or slides will land when you release the mouse button. On the Slides pane, a horizontal line appears between slides to show you where the slide or slides will land when you release the mouse button.
- ❑ **Cutting and pasting:** On the Home tab, cut the slide or slides to the Windows Clipboard (click the Cut button, press Ctrl+X, or right-click and choose Cut). Then select the slide that you want the slide or slides to appear after and give the Paste command (click the Paste button, press Ctrl+V, or right-click and choose Paste). You can right-click between slides to paste with precision.

Deleting slides

Select the slide or slides you want to delete and use one of these methods to delete slides:

- ✓ Press the Delete key.
- ✓ Right-click and choose Delete Slide on the shortcut menu.

Points to Remember

- ☞ Before finalizing your slideshow, review it on your system
- ☞ Select slides setup according to your need
- ☞ Save a presentation style as template you like

Let's Start PowerPoint

In this chapter you will learn

- Selecting theme for your presentation
- Creating background & designs for your presentation
- Customising the slide appearance
- Editing the Slide styles

Choosing a Theme for Your Presentation

After you initially select a theme, you can do one or two things to customize it. These pages explain how to find and select a theme for your presentation and diddle with a theme after you select it. By the way, the name of the theme that is currently in use is listed on the left side of the status bar, in case you're curious about a theme you want to replace.

Selecting a theme

Use one of these methods to select a new theme for your presentation:

❑ **Selecting a theme in the Themes gallery:** On the Design tab, open the Themes gallery and move the pointer over different themes to "live preview" them. Click a theme to select it.

❑ **Borrowing a theme from another presentation:** On the Design tab, open the Themes gallery, and click Browse for Themes. Select and click the Apply button.

Tweaking a theme

Starting on the Design tab, you can customize a theme with these techniques and in so doing alter all the slides in your presentation:

❑ **Choosing a new set of colours:** The easiest and best way to experiment with customizing a theme is to select a different colour set. Click the Colours button, slide the pointer over the different colour sets on the dropdown list, and see what effect they have on your slides.

❑ **Change the fonts:** Click the Fonts button and choose a font combination on the drop-down list. The first font in each pair applies to slide titles and the second to slide text. You can also choose Create New Theme Fonts on the list and select theme fonts of your own.

❑ **Change theme effects:** Click the Effects button and choose a theme effect on the drop-down list. A theme effect is a slight refinement to a theme.

❑ **Choosing background style variation:** Most themes offer background style variations. Click the Background Styles button to open the Background Styles gallery and select a style.

Creating Slide Backgrounds on Your Own

Besides a theme or background style, your other option for creating slide backgrounds is to do it on your own. For a background, you can have a solid colour, a transparent colour, a gradient blend of colours, a picture, or a clip-artimage.

❑ **Solid colour:** A single, uniform colour. You can adjust a colour's transparency and in effect "bleach out" the colour to push it farther into the background.

❑ **Gradient:** A mixture of different colours with the colours blending into one another.

❑ **Clip art:** A clip-art image from the Microsoft Clip Organizer.

❑ **Picture:** A photograph or graphic.

❑ **Texture:** A uniform pattern that gives the impression that the slide is displayed on a material such as cloth or stone.

Using a solid (or transparent) colour for the slide background

Follow these steps to use a solid or transparent colour as the background for slides:

✓ On the Design tab, click the Background Styles button and choose Format Background on the drop-down list. You see the Fill category of the Format Background dialog box.

- ✓ Select the Solid Fill option button.

- ✓ Click the Colour button and choose a colour on the drop-down list. The muted theme colours are recommended because they look better in the background, but you can select a standard colour or click the More Colours button and select a colour in the Colours dialog box.

- ✓ Drag the Transparency slider if you want a "bleached out" colour rather than a slide colour. At 0% transparency, you get a solid colour; at 100%, you get no colour at all.

- ✓ Click the Apply to All button and then the Close button.

Follow these steps to create a gradient background for slides:

- ✓ On the Design tab, click the Background Styles button, and choose Format Background on the drop-down list. You see the Fill category of the Format Background dialog box. Drag this dialog box to the left side of the screen so that you can get a better view of your slide.

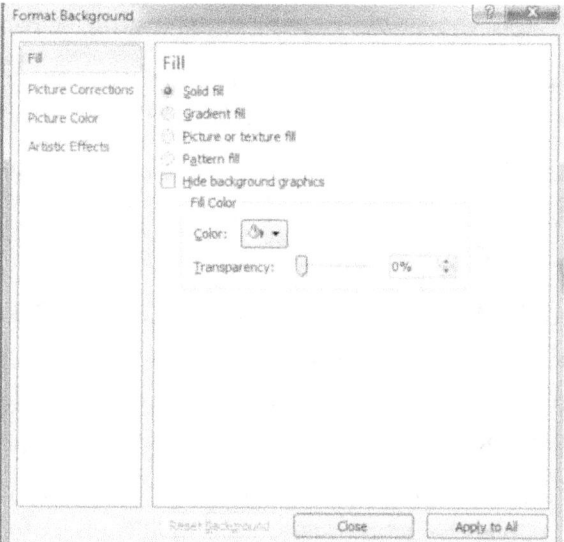

Creating gradient background

- ✓ Click the Gradient Fill option button.

- ✓ On the Type drop-down list, choose what type of gradient you want — Linear, Radial, Rectangular, Path, or Shade from Title. If you choose Linear, you can enter a degree measurement in the Angle box to change the angle at which the colours blend. At 90 degrees, for example, colours blend horizontally across the slide; at 180 degrees, they blend vertically.

- ✓ Create a gradient stop for each colour transition you want on yourslides. Gradient stops determine where colours are, how colours transition fromone to the next, and which colours are used. You can create as many gradient stops as you want. Here are methods for handling gradient stops:

  - ❑ **Adding a gradient stop:** Click the Add Gradient Stop button. A new gradient stop appears on the slider. Drag it to where you want the colour blend to occur.

  - ❑ **Removing a gradient stop:** Select a gradient stop on the slider and click the Remove Gradient Stop button.

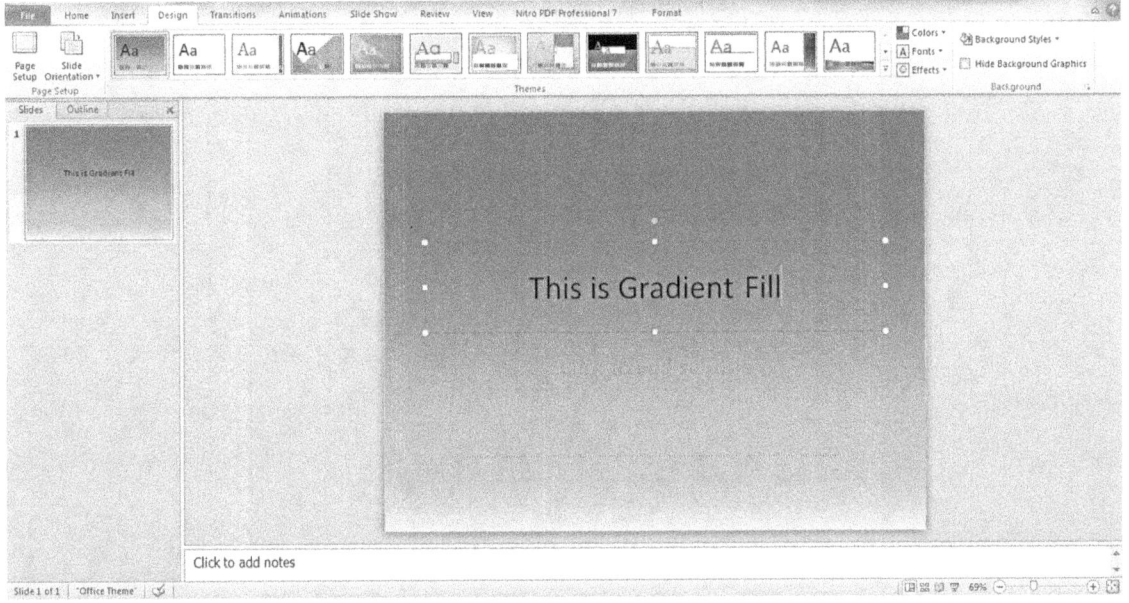

- ❏ **Choosing a colour for a gradient stop:** Select a gradient stop on the slider, click the Colour button, and choose a colour on the drop-down list.

- ❏ **Positioning a gradient stop:** Drag a gradient stop on the slider or use the Position box to move it to a different location.

- ❏ Drag the Brightness slider to make the colours dimmer or brighter.

Creating Slide Backgrounds on Your Own

Drag the Transparency slider to make the colours on the slides more or less transparent. At 0% transparency, you get solid colours; at 100%, you get no colour at all. Click the Apply to All button.

Placing a clip-art image in the slide background

- ✓ On the Design tab, click the Background Styles button and choose Format Background on the drop-down list. The Fill category of the Format Background dialog box appears

- ✓ Click the Picture or Texture Fill option button.

- ✓ Click the Clip Art button. You see the Select Picture dialog box.

- ✓ Find and select a clip-art image that you can use in the background of your slides. You can scroll through the clip-art images until you find a good one, enter a search term in the Search Text

box and click the Go button (click the Include Content from Office Online check box to search online at Microsoft for a clip-art image), or click the Import button to get an image from your computer.

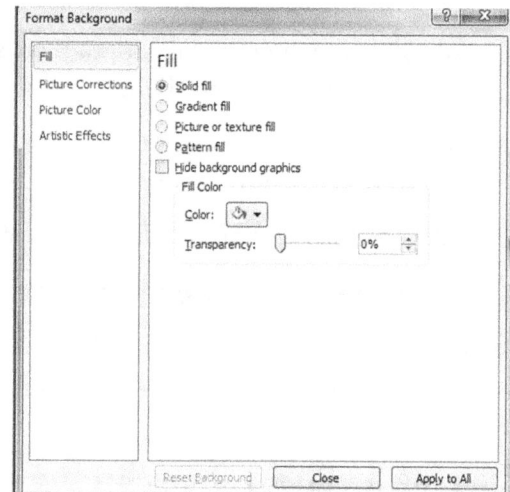

✓ In the Format Background dialog box, enter a Transparency measurement. Drag the Transparency slider or enter a measurement in the box. The higher the measurement, the more transparent the image is.

✓ Enter measurements in the Offsets boxes to make your clip-art image fill the slide.

✓ Click the Apply to All button and then click Close.

Formatting background

Follow these steps to use a picture as a slide background:

✓ On the Design tab, click the Background Styles button and choose Format Background on the drop-down list. You see the Fill category of the Format Background dialog box.

✓ Click the Picture or Texture Fill option button.

✓ Click the File tab. The Insert Picture dialog box appears.

✓ Locate the picture you want, select it, and click the Insert button. The picture lands on your slide.

✓ Enter a Transparency measurement to make the picture fade a bit in to the background. Using the Offsets text boxes, enter measurements to make your picturefit on the slides.

✓ Click the Apply to All button.

Using a texture for a slide background

✓ On the Design tab, click the Background Styles button and choose Format Background on the drop-down list.

✓ Click the Picture or Texture Fill option button.

✓ Click the Texture button and choose a texture on the drop-down list.

✓ Enter a Transparency measurement to make the texture less imposing.

✓ Drag the slider or enter a measurement in the Transparency box.

✓ Click the Apply to All button and then click Close.

Points to Remember

☞ Create all formatting on the frame only, since any formatting done outside the frame will be unavailable during slide show
☞ Choose colours and other formatting elements wisely

Text &Text Boxes

In this chapter you will learn

- Entering text
- Using Custom Text Boxes

Entering Text

Here we will discuss how to enter text in a slide in a Powerpoint presentation.

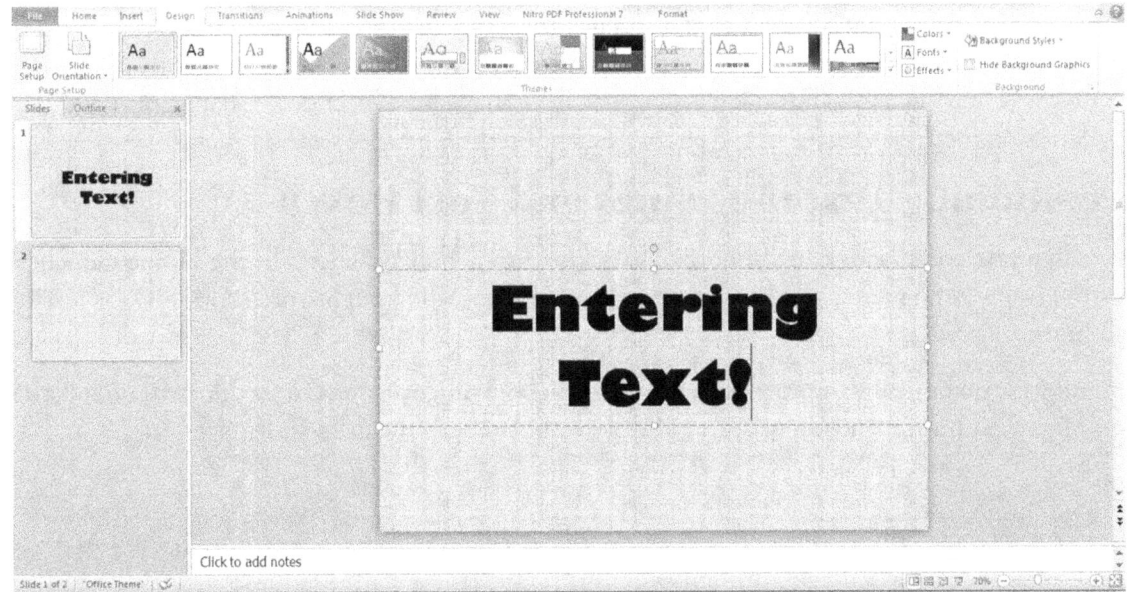

Text Boxes and Text Box Shapes

❑ **Creating a text box:** On the Insert tab, click the Text Box button and move the pointer to a part of the slide where you can see the text box pointer, a downward-pointing arrow. Then click and start dragging to create your text box, and enter the text.

❑ **Filling a text box with a colour style:** On the (Drawing Tools) Format tab, choose a style on the Shape Styles gallery.

❑ **Rotating a text box (text included):** Use one of these techniques to rotate a text box along with the text inside it:

   ✓ Drag the rotation handle, the green circle above the text box.

   ✓ On the (Drawing Tools) Format tab, click the Rotate button and choose a Rotate or Flip command on the drop-down list.

   ✓ On the (Drawing Tools) Format tab, click the Size group button (you may have to click the Size button first) and, in the Size category of the Format Shape dialog box, enter a measurement in the Rotation box.

❑ **Turning a shape into a text box:** Create the shape, and then click in the shape and start typing.

❑ **Turning a text box into a shape:** Right-click the text box and choose Format Shape. In the Format Shape dialog box, click the Text Box category and under AutoFit, click the Do Not AutoFit option button. Then close the dialog box, go to the (Drawing Tools) Format tab, click the Edit Shape button, choose Change Shape on the drop-down list, and choose a shape on the Change Shape submenu.

Positioning Text in Frames and Text Boxes

   ✓ Align text commands control horizontal (left-to-right) alignments. On the Home tab, click the Align Left (press Ctrl+L), Center (press Ctrl+E), Align Right (press Ctrl+R), or Justify button.

   ✓ Align Text commands control vertical (up-and-down) alignments. On the Home tab, click the Align Text button and choose Top, Middle, or Bottom on the drop-down list.

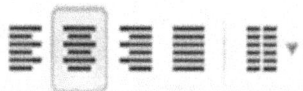

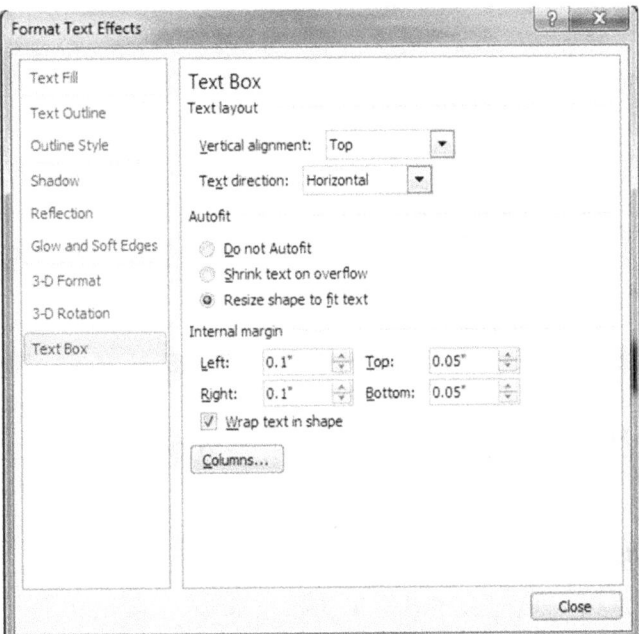

Format text effects

Points to Remember

☞ Place the text box in the frame only, it will not appear out of the frame during slide show

12th

Chapter

Transitions & Animations

In this chapter you will learn

- Using Animations in Slide show
- Using Transitions to slides
- Inserting Sound & Video clips in presentation
- Converting presentation into Video

In PowerPoint, a transition is a little bit of excitement that occurs as one slide leaves the screen and the next slide climbs aboard. An animation is movement on the slide.

Tools for tweaking a transition:

❏ **Effect Options:** Click the Effect Options button and choose an effect on the drop-down list. For example, choose From Top or From Bottom to make a transition arrive from the top or bottom of the screen. Not all transitions offer effect options.

❏ **Sound:** Open the Sound drop-down list and choose a sound to accompany the transition. The Loop Until Next Sound option at the bottom of the drop-down list plays a sound continuously until the next slide in the presentation appears.

❏ **Duration:** Enter a time period in the Duration box to declare how quickly or slowly you want the transition to occur. As mentioned earlier, you can click the Apply To All button to assign the same.

Altering and removing slide transitions

In the Slides pane and Slide Sorter view, the transition symbol, a flying star, appears next to slides that have been assigned a transition. Select the slides that need a transition change, go to the Transitions tab, and follow these instructions to alter or remove transitions:

❑ **Altering a transition:** Choose a different transition in the Transition to This Slide gallery. You can also choose different effect options and sounds, and change the duration of the transition.

❑ **Removing a transition:** Choose None in the Transition to This Slide gallery.

Animating parts of a slide

Follow these steps to preview and choose an animation scheme for slides:

✓ Go to the Animations tab.

✓ Click to select the element on the slide that you want to animate. For example, select a text frame with a bulleted list. You can tell when you've selected an element because a selection box appears around it.

✓ In the Animation Styles gallery, choose an animation effect.

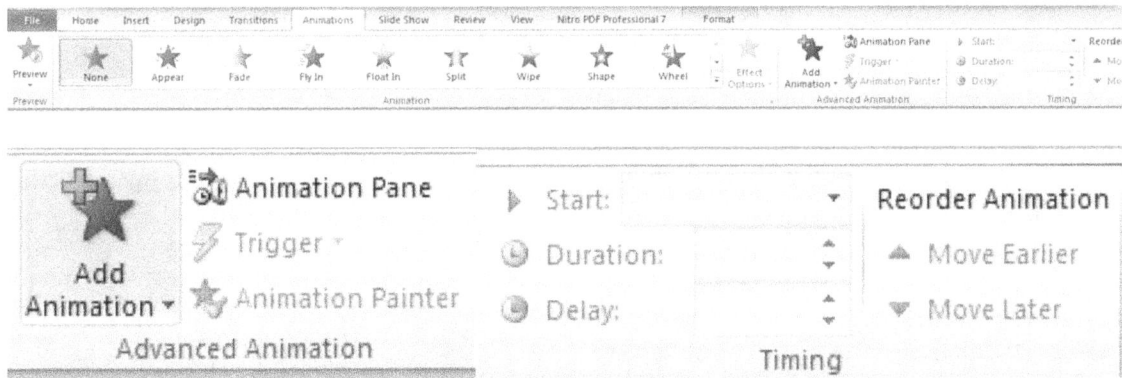

You can choose Entrance, Emphasis, and Exit animation effects. As soon as you make your choice, the animation springs to life, and you can click the Preview button at any time to see your animation in all its glory.

✓ Click the Effect Options button and experiment with choices on the drop-down list to tweak your animation. Which options are available depends on the animation you chose.

✓ **All at Once:** All the text is animated at the same time.

✓ **By Paragraph:** Each paragraph is treated separately and is animated on its own.

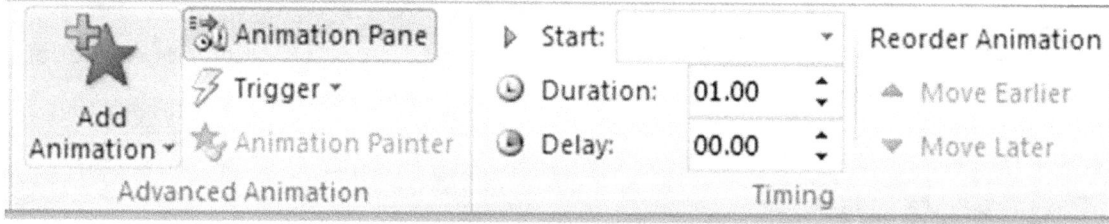

To remove an animation, return to the Animation Styles gallery and choose None.

Audio Part of Your Presentation

PowerPoint offers two ways to make audio part of a presentation:

❑ **As part of slide transitions:** A sound is heard as a new slide arrives on-screen. On the Transitions tab, open the Sound drop-down list and choose a sound.

☐ **On the slide itself:** The means of playing audio appears on the slide in the form of an Audio icon. By moving the mouse over this icon, you can display audio controls, and you can use these controls to play audio. You can also make audio play as soon as the slide arrives on-screen.

Audio

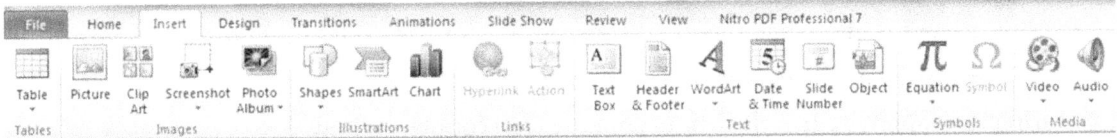

Inserting an audio file on a slide

Follow these steps to insert an audio file in a slide:

✓ Go to the Insert tab.

✓ Click the Audio button. You will see the Insert Audio dialog box.

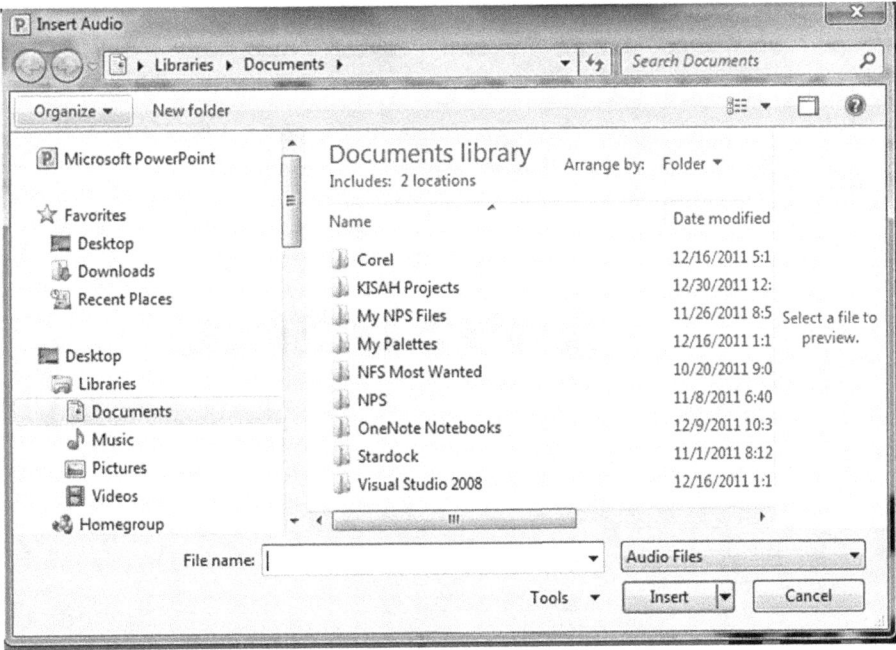

✓ Locate and select a sound file and then click Insert.

Playing audio during a presentation

While an audio file is playing during a presentation, controls for starting, pausing, and controlling the volume appear on-screen.

Follow these instructions to start, pause, and control the volume of an audio recording during a presentation:

❏ **Starting an audio file:** Move the pointer over the Audio icon, and when you see the Audio controls, click the Play/Pause button (or press Alt+P).

❏ **Pausing an audio file:** Click the Play/Pause button (or press Alt+P). Click the button again to resume playing the audio file.

❏ **Muting the volume:** Click the Mute/Unmute icon (or press Alt+U).

❏ **Controlling the volume:** Move the pointer over the Mute/Unmute icon to display the volume slider and then drag the volume control on the slider.

Inserting a video on a slide

Follow these steps to insert a video on a slide:

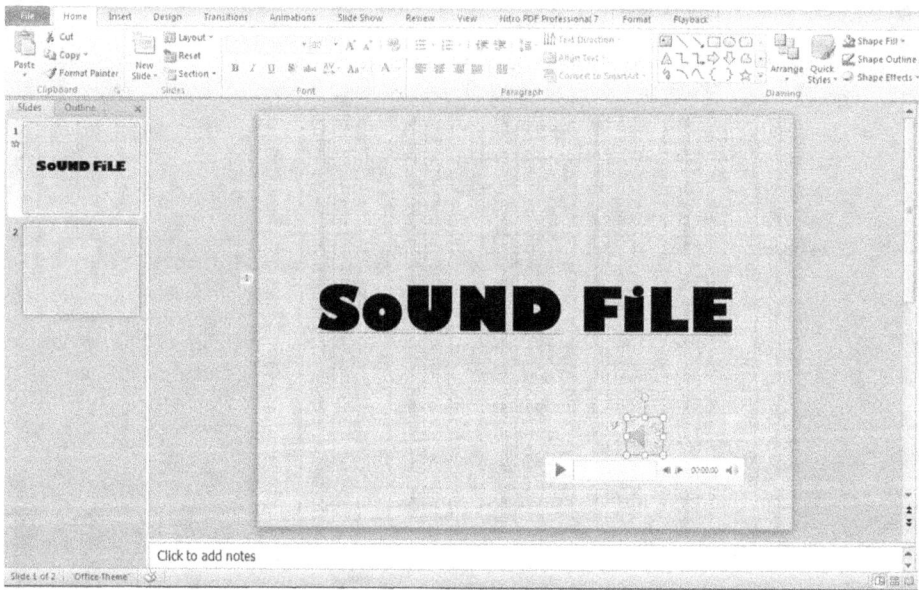

❏ Open the Insert Video dialog box. You can open the dialog box with one of these methods:

    ✓ Click the Media icon in a content place holder frame.

    ✓ On the Insert tab, click the Video button.

❑ Select a video file in the Insert Video dialog box and click Insert.

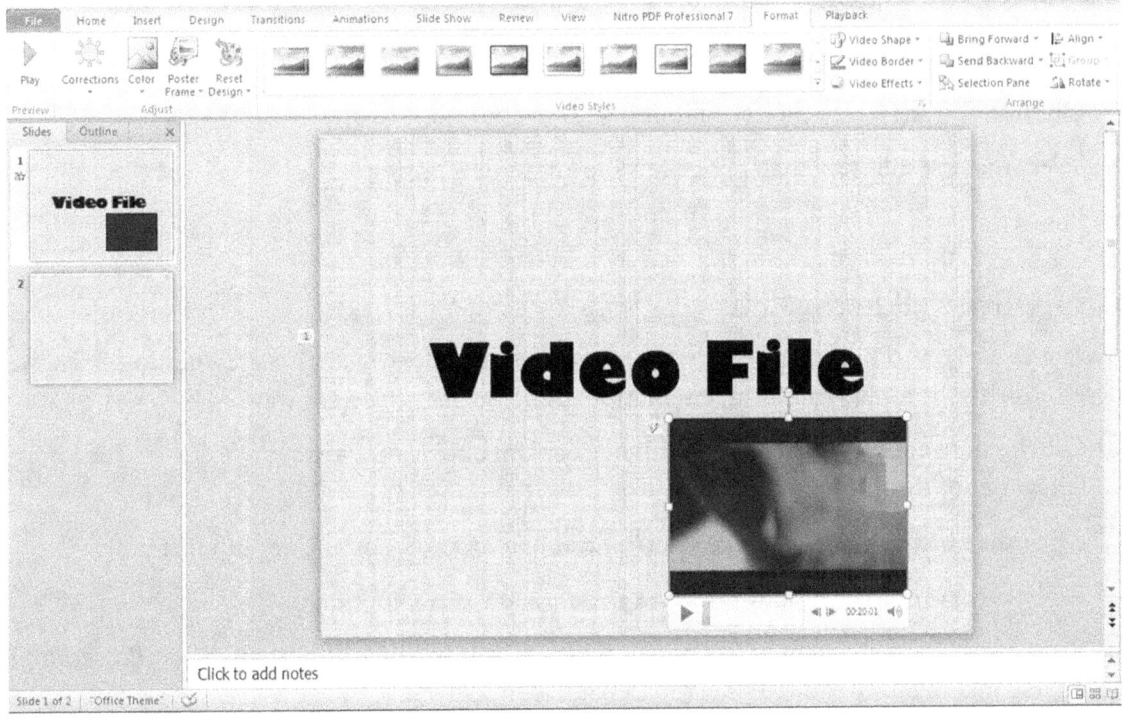

❑ **Controlling the volume:** Click the Volume button and choose Low, Medium, High, or Mute to control how loud the video sound is.

❑ **Playing the video automatically or when you click the Play/Pause button:** Open the Start drop-down list and choose Automatically or On Click to tell PowerPoint when to start playing the video.

❑ **Playing the video at full screen:** Make a video fill the entire screen by selecting the Play Full Screen check box. Be careful of this one. Videos can look terribly grainy when they appear on the big screen.

❑ **Hiding the video when it isn't playing:** You can hide the video until you start playing it by selecting the Hide While Not Playing check box. Be sure to choose Automatically on the Start drop-down list if you select this check box.

❑ **Continuously playing, or looping the video:** Play a video continuously or until you go to the next slide by selecting the Loop Until Stopped check box.

- ❑ **Rewinding the video when it's finished playing:** Rewind a video if you want to see the first frame, not the last, when the video finishes playing.

Showing Your Presentation

- ✓ On the Slide Show tab, click the From Beginning button.
- ✓ Select the first slide and then click the Slide Show view button
- ✓ Press F5

Going fro slide to slide

In a nutshell, PowerPoint offers four ways to move from slide to slide in a presentation. Here we describe methods for navigating a presentation, using the four different ways:

- ❑ **Use the slide control buttons:** Click a slide control button — Previous, Next — in the lower-left corner of the screen.

- ❑ **Click the Slide button:** Click this button and make a choice on the pop-up menu.

- ❑ **Right-click on-screen:** Right-click and choose a navigation option on the shortcut menu.

- ❑ **Press a keyboard shortcut:** Press one of the numerous keyboard shortcuts. That PowerPoint offers for going from slide to slide (Spacebar, PgUp, PgDn...)

Wielding a pen or highlighter in a presentation

Follow these instructions so that you can draw on a slide:

- ❑ **Selecting a pen or highlighter:** PowerPoint offers Pen for writing on slides and Highlighter for highlighting text on slides. To select the Pen or Highlighter, click the Pen button and choose Pen or Highlighter. You can also right-click, choose Pointer Options, and make a selection on the submenu.

- ❑ **Choosing a colour for drawing:** After you select the Pen or Highlighter, click the Pen button, choose Ink Colour, and select a colour on the submenu

Follow these steps to make yours a kiosk-style, self-running presentation:
- ✓ Go to the Slide Show tab.
- ✓ Click the Set Up Slide Show button.

You will see the Set Up Slide Show dialog box.

✓ Under Show Type, select the Browsed at a Kiosk (Full Screen) option. When you select this option, PowerPoint automatically selects the Loop Continuously Until 'Esc' check box.

✓ Make sure that the Using Timings, If Present option button is selected.

✓ Click OK.

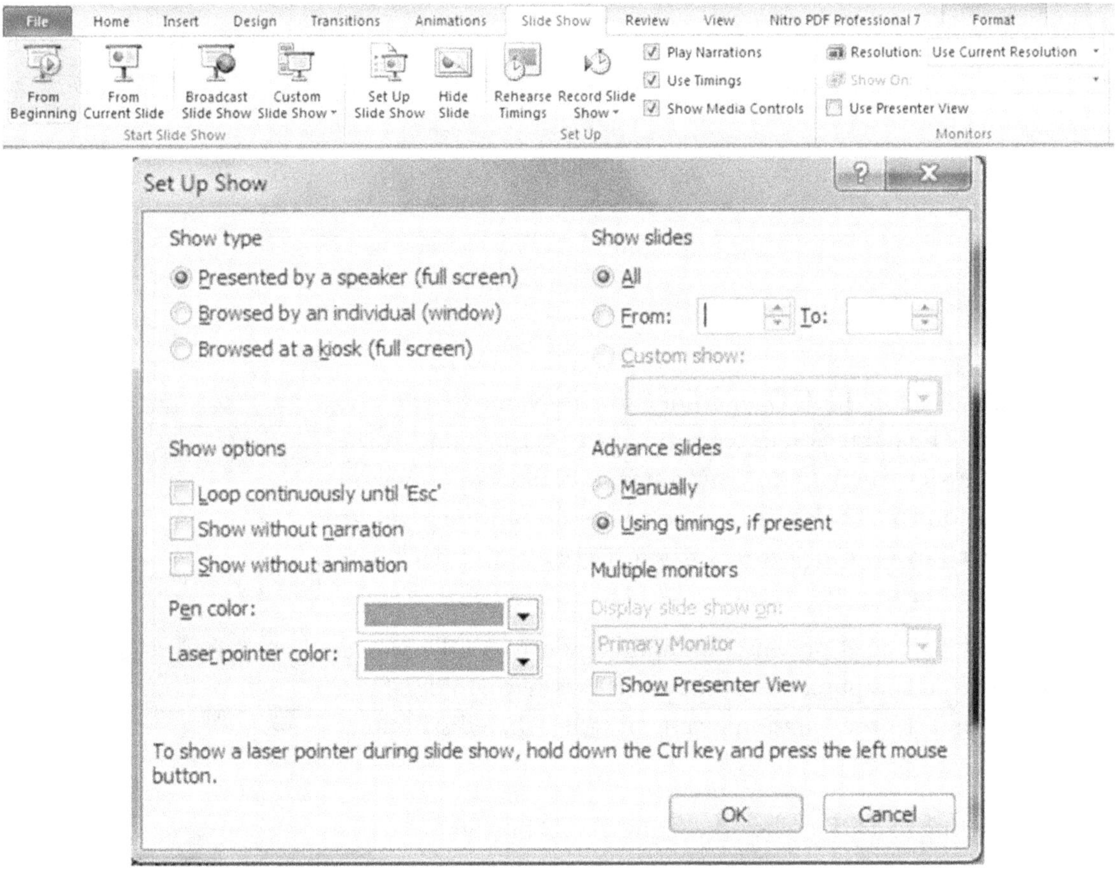

Packaging a presentation on a CD

Follow these steps to copy your presentation and the PowerPoint Viewer to a CD or a folder:

✓ Open the presentation you want to package.

✓ On the File tab, choose Save & Send.

✓ Choose Package Presentation for CD, and click the Package for CD button.

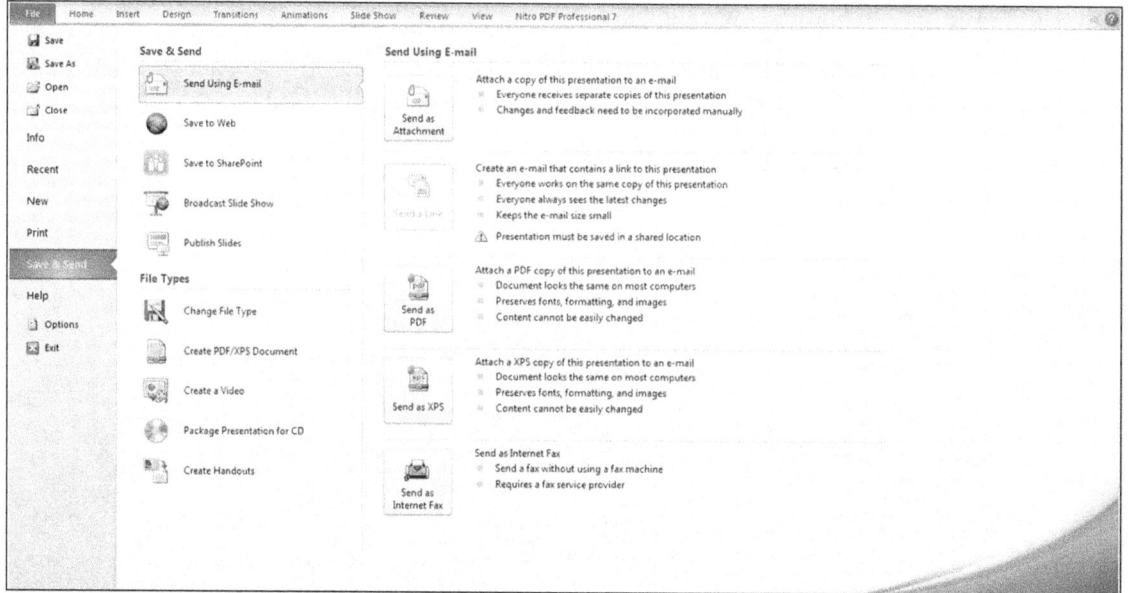

✓ Enter a name for the CD or folder in the Name of the CD text box. The name you enter will appear as the name of the CD if you view the CD on Computer; if you're copying your presentation to a folder, the name you enter will be given to the folder PowerPoint creates when it creates the packaged presentation file.

✓ Create the packaged presentation and copy it to a CD or to a folder on your computer. Copy the presentation to a folder if you want to send the presentation by e-mail rather than distribute it by CD.

❑ **Copying to a CD:** Click the Copy to CD button.

❑ **Copying to a folder:** Click the Copy to Folder button. In the Copy to Folder dialog box, click the Browse button, and in the ChooseLocation dialog box, select a folder for storing the folder where you will keep your packaged presentation. Then click the Select button and click OK in the Copy to Folder dialog box.

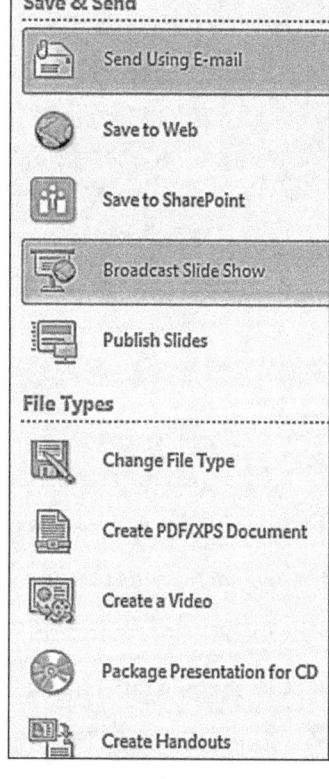

✓ Click Yes in the message box that asks if you want to include linked content in the presentation. It can take PowerPoint several minutes to assemble the files and copy them to the CD or folder.

Creating a presentation video

Follow these steps to create a WMV-file version of a PowerPoint presentation:

✓ On the File tab, choose Save & Send.

✓ Choose Create a Video. You see the Create a Video window.

✓ Open the first drop-down list and choose a display resolution for your video.

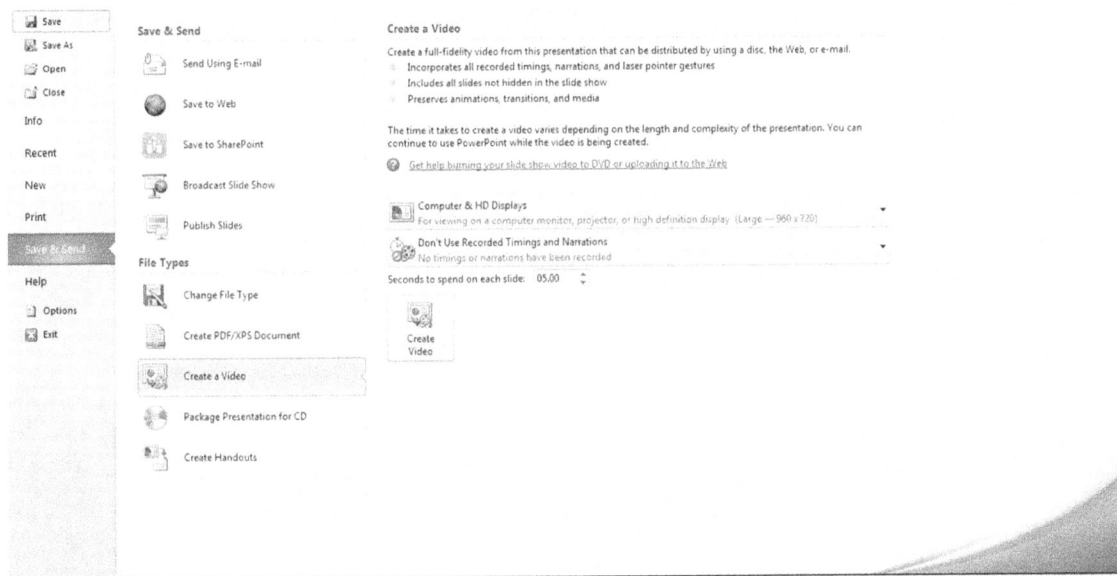

✓ Open the second drop-down list and choose whether to use recorded timings and narrations.

✓ Open the second drop-down list and choose Preview Timings and Narrations. Your presentation video plays. How do you like it? This is what your video will look and sound like after you save it in a WMV file.

✓ Click the Create Video button. The Save As dialog box opens.

✓ Choose a folder for storing the WMV file, enter a name for the file, and click the Save button.

Points to Remember

☞ Use Animation & transition with tools to ensure that which object will appear on click & which will appear automatically

☞ Use suitable frame for videos

☞ Your Sound clip button should appear on frame during slide show

☞ While converting the file into Video, please set the sound clips & Video playback in auto-mode by setting time limits.

www.ingramcontent.com/pod-product-compliance
Lightning Source LLC
Chambersburg PA
CBHW080739250626
47170CB00010B/2890